An Inch
In Time

An Inch
In Time

THE STORY OF JUSTIN JOLLIE OLIVER INCH

● ● ●

Denise Pinhey

ISBN: 1522756701
ISBN 13: 9781522756705
Library of Congress Control Number: 2016912166
CreateSpace Independent Publishing Platform
North Charleston, South Carolina

CHAPTER 1
Justin Jollie Oliver Inch

● ● ●

WHEN JUSTIN DROVE HIS '98 Chevy into a semi truck, transporting used grease from McDonald's, the grease exploded, a French-fry smell filled the air, and Justin disappeared into a spectacular fireball of oil and ash. It was a great show, and he never tired of watching it. The accident always ended with fascinated onlookers driving slowly by the smoking wreckage. Cell phones in hand, they bragged about what they saw. It caused a huge traffic jam, but people waited patiently for their turns to take a look. Justin's death made national news and was the most popular video on YouTube for six months.

"And to think I made it happen without sneaking a gun into a high school, robbing a widow, or living in a tree as part of a social protest," he marveled. "True genius always leaves its tracks. It is only a matter of time until others discover who made the footprints."

Justin leaned out of the arched opening of the cloud to see better.

Justin had been dead for twenty years now. He wore a faded blue hospital gown and a beautiful Hermes tie. Justin stroked the smooth red silk that hung around his neck.

He looked exactly the same as he always had—brown and ordinary. He had brown eyes and brown hair. He was five-foot nine, and weighed one hundred and sixty-five pounds. He was thirty-three years old. He would be thirty-three forever.

The video ended. Justin hung his head upside down over the edge of the cloud into the dark space to enjoy the terror of watching the earth zoom away. When it finished, he sat up.

"Heaven is the loneliest place on earth," he said to nobody, "because creativity in its purest form is born of nothing—I should write that down." He poked his index finger into the cloud fluff and began writing. The letters always filled over as soon as he took his finger away, but he did it anyway. After the last letter disappeared, he turned around and stared out into the surprising activity.

Far below, surrounded by Christmas tree lights and spaceship garbage, the dizzy blue earth spun on its mystery axis. A space shuttle wandered aimlessly by, and suns, planets, and meteor showers pinned the icy blanket of darkness and kept it from floating away. Justin brushed a hand across his face, searching for a tear but finding none.

"People look like ants, buildings look like blocks of cheese, and cars look like cockroaches—what a sad, sad world it is." Justin hugged himself and sighed.

Justin's real name was Justin Oliver Inch—Justin Inch. For years, people made fun of him. The jokes began in junior high. Even the girls joined in.

They called him Justin Inch because
Justin Inch was all there was.

In high school, the taunts became more sophisticated, expanding to four lines instead of two.

They called him Justin Inch because
Justin Inch was all there was
When he finally got a date
What he gave her was cut-rate.

After he started working, the ridicule became more subtle. Its subtlety bothered him most of all. He couldn't respond to it without looking like he was making a big deal out of nothing. The method his tormenters used was clever but effective. Coworkers simply called him by his first and last name.

"Good morning, Justin Inch."

"Justin Inch, can I borrow your stapler?"

"You're late, Justin Inch."

No matter what form the comments took, the message was always the same. It was nothing really, an old joke, but he was damn sick of it. Justin kicked at the cloud fluff that was too mushy to give satisfaction.

Justin gazed dully at the thick white fluffs of cotton that formed the wall of his cloud cave. The fluff both comforted and smothered; it ran up the curved walls and covered the dome ceiling. The floor was heavy with even thicker layers of the same silky mush. The stuff looked like it should taste like cotton candy but it had no flavor.

"It looks sticky too," Justin commented, picking at a bit of the goo and flicking it out. The gunk disappeared into limitless, terrifying space.

He meditated on the cupcake-sized red button mounted on a gold stand that tilted to one side because the cloud fluff could not anchor it properly. His mood brightened.

"A great thing, that button," Justin said to himself.

And so it was. By pushing the red button, he could watch anything that ever happened on earth. He could see dinosaurs play, study the rise and fall of the Roman Empire, or savor Napoleon and Josephine frolicking in the royal bed. He could go centuries back into the past or centuries forward into the future, but he never bothered with these. Instead, he watched himself.

Justin hesitated a moment to let his hand float above the cupcake button before pressing it. He had pressed the button thousands of times. It always gave him a tiny electric shock that he never got used to. He prepared himself and leaned out the arched door of the cloud. The cold, black space outside was vast enough to hold all possibility. A hushed moment, and then his fingers grabbed the familiar red sponge. The button was soft and warm at first; it begged to be squeezed. Then it delivered its tiny shock, Justin felt the cloud jerk forward, and his heart vaulted into his throat.

Fast as he traveled, the world was a long, long way off. It would have made more sense to relocate the cloud closer, but as soon as the video ended, the world sped away until it was the size of a gumball, and he had to start the trip from the beginning again. It took an entire fifteen minutes to get close enough to see the shapes of the continents. He recognized South America by its elephant-shaped head. Africa was a horse's head. The tornado was North America, and Europe and Asia made a huge, carnivorous parrot that swooped down with outstretched wings to capture a fleeing Australian butterfly. After exactly five minutes, Justin could see the sock that was California. It took only one minute for California to splinter into tangled electric freeways, saltine boxes, and dotted parking lots, and then cities gave way to fewer cities that gave way to the city of Oakland, specifically, the southwest side, where Justin grew up. Oakland was in the East Bay, twelve miles from San Francisco, or an hour in commute traffic. Now, he could pick out his family's dirt-beige, flat-topped tract house. Finally, Justin saw the tiny inhabitants.

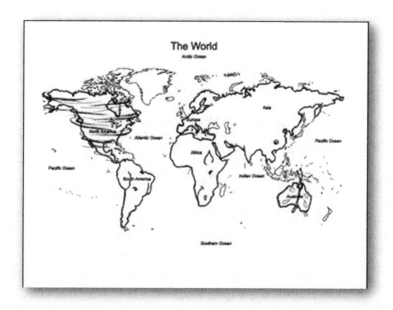

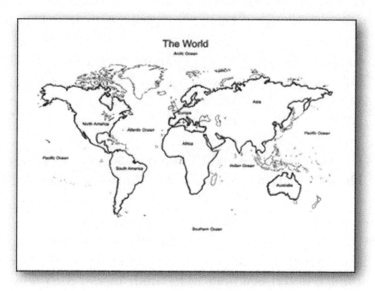

CHAPTER 2

What Child Is This

● ● ●

THE VIDEO ALWAYS STARTED ON a Wednesday morning at exactly nine o'clock on July 10, a month after Justin turned eight years old. Most people had already left for work, but Justin's father, Clyde Inch, was usually home because his business was building malls, and malls had gone out of style when people had taken to shopping at Allmart instead. Allmart's prices were cheaper, and the merchandise was the same from store to store, so you knew exactly what to expect. The Inches did all right though. Neither parent had grown up with money, so being broke was perfectly acceptable. His mother worked nights delivering pizzas and did surprisingly pretty well. People were not used to having a woman delivering their pizza, and they liked the effect. It was like having Mom drop by to fix you dinner.

Justin always walked alone to school. He liked walking alone, liked looking at people's houses and thinking about the people who lived in them. The white house belonged to Mr. Finkle, who turned the sprinklers on so the kids wouldn't skate up and down in front of his house. The old woman who smelled like unwashed socks and liked to wave out the window lived in the blue house. His sometimes-friend, Jeremy, lived in the crabgrass house on the corner. He must have had parents, but Justin had never seen them. The Smits owned the yellow house— they had four new plastic trashcans, all of them with "Smit" written on the side in big, black letters. Justin walked two more blocks. He was almost to school.

Dostoevsky Elementary School was a slap-hazard affair made up of ten trailers that housed twenty classes of children, ages five to eleven. The trailers formed a semicircle that abutted a wall the kids used for playing handball. In the center space, a swing, a slide, and a hopscotch area made a playground. In addition to the classrooms, each trailer had two bathrooms and a drinking fountain. There was a city park only a block away, but the city had barred the children from going there because they would not obey the Keep off the Grass signs.

Justin skipped into trailer twenty-five B, his third grade classroom.

The teacher's name was Ms. Big Sky. She was a round mountain of a woman with a beautiful olive complexion and impossibly shiny hair. Ms. Big Sky took great pride in how she decorated her classroom. The children made everything. Papier-Mache mice lined the bookcases, glittery somethings hung from the ceiling, Christmas chains of cheap colored paper framed the windows. There were prize-winning crayon pictures, Popsicle-stick men, and there were—oh, so many things. Suffice it to say, the room was a chaotic, happy mess, and the children loved it because it was just like home.

Once a week, Ms. Big Sky selected a few students to read their writing assignments aloud. The readings allowed even the stupidest child to be a star, if only for a few minutes. Ms. Big Sky was always careful to dole out her attentions equally. Had she accidently praised the high achievers more, the other kids would have beaten them up during recess.

Twenty-five eight-year-olds sat cross-legged on a ratty green rug, brightened with multicolored crayon scribbles. They tumbled and rocked. To prevent their escape, Ms. Big Sky had taught them to stay inside the rug's borders. It was paper-sharing time, the best part of the best day of the week. The kids loved listening to the stories, no matter how terrible they were, and they sat quietly, their eyes shining with expectation.

A sticky-mouthed, dirty-necked little boy stood in front of the gaggle of children, holding a single page of graphite-smudged paper. He was eight years old, a skinny pale kid in baggy pants and a rumpled T-shirt. Overwhelmed with excitement, he kept grabbing his crotch.

"There I am," Justin said in admiration from his cloud. "Justin Oliver Inch."

The little boy took a deep breath and shouted, "My name is Justin Inch, and the name of my story is 'My Best Friend'—by Justin Inch."

"Inside voice, Justin," Ms. Big Sky reminded him.

"Uh-huh. Me and my friend, we were walking to school. We are both eight years old, so we can walk by ourselves. We were almost to the dogs. There are two of them."

The children wiggled with excitement at the mention of the dogs. Some barked.

Justin caught their enthusiasm and his sticky hands began crumpling his paper.

"The dogs, they live behind a fence, and they always bark and try to bite people who walk by. Those dogs are mean, and they like it that way. I try to poke them with sticks."

Laughter from the children. Some fell on their backs and kicked, being careful to stay on the rug. Justin danced and swiped at an imaginary dog with an imaginary stick.

"When I poke the dogs through the fence, it makes them all wild. Those dogs hate me because I am mean to them because they are just stupid dogs, and I am a smart boy. That time, when I was walking with my friend, the dogs got out by a hole in the fence."

Now the children sat still, transfixed by danger and suspense.

"Me and my friend, we ran as fast as we could. We jumped over bushes, and the biting, barking dogs ran after us. We ran to the big tree in Mr. Betty's yard. I could run faster, so I was the first to climb up, and I kept climbing higher and higher."

Huge excitement. Tommy hooted, Jennie rolled, and Randy growled and snapped his teeth at the air. Christie caught a scratch and kicked Samantha. Bobbie jumped on Joey, who kicked Carrie's leg. A snarl of elbows, arms, tennis shoes, and accusations tumbled and fought within the confines of the rug. Ms. Big Sky marched to the chalkboard and began writing names. Calm blessed the classroom.

"Go ahead, Justin," Ms. Big Sky said after they had all settled down. The kids remembered the dogs and stared ahead, wanting more. Justin continued.

"My friend climbed as far up as he could. I could hear him yelling, 'Shit! Climb, Justin! Climb!'"

"Justin—we do not use that kind of language."

"My father does. He says shit a whole lot." Justin said with all the indignity of an eight-year-old who has caught a grown-up in a lie.

"My mom says it, and she says the f-word too," said Billy. The kids stared disapprovingly at Ms. Big Sky.

Further emboldened by Ms. Big Sky's betrayal, Justin continued. His paper was a soggy mass, wet with child's sweat and mayonnaise.

"My friend knew he was going to die, and he wanted me to live."

The children absorbed the drama. Some held hands. It was easy to love a best friend, even one you had just met yesterday. The rug became a warm nest full of beautiful children.

"Mr. Betty, he was damn mad about the noise in his front yard, and he left the TV on and went out to see. When he saw us in his tree and the dogs trying to bite us, I think he was glad because it was exciting, and his wife is dead. Then he dialed emergency nine one one on his cell phone. He was yelling. 'Come quick! There are two big, mean dogs in my front yard trying to kill two boys in a tree!' But they wouldn't come because Mr. Betty didn't know our names. So Mr. Betty lied."

All of the kids turned to look at Ms. Big Sky, who had lied only a minute ago.

"Mr. Betty told the emergency lady, 'I thought two boys were in a tree but really my house is on fire.'" Then he yelled at us again. 'They're sending the fire department!' he said. 'I told them the house was on fire!' I yelled back, 'You're stupid, and you have a girl's name!'"

The children's voices collided in laughter and the kids rolled, shouted, and kicked one another. Again, they were careful to stay on the rug.

Justin wiggled and danced. His joke about Mr. Betty's name had gone well.

"My friend was in the tree but not high enough, and he was kicking the dogs."

Justin demonstrated by a kick toward the other children, but not before they could jump back in a huddled squeal.

"Inside voice, Justin," Ms. Big Sky cautioned.

"When the firemen came, the dogs already pulled my friend down. The dogs tore him up into little red pieces of dog food, and the firemen chopped the dogs to death with their axes."

That started it. Unable to contain their excitement, children broke free from the rug. They ran to the back of the classroom, shouting and flailing at one another. Ms. Big Sky corralled and herded them back into the confines of the rug, where they continued the melee.

"My!" Ms. Big Sky said. "I like how Janie is sitting so nice and quiet. She is my favorite little girl."

The kids crossed their legs, folded their hands, and sat up straight. Their eyes begged for their teacher's notice.

Justin had lost the children's attention. His head dropped, and he wrapped it up. "The firemen helped me out of the tree. They were very nice and careful not to hurt me. It was my best friend that died."

The kids' tiny hands clapped a jerky rhythm of appreciation. Justin handed his soggy glob of paper to Ms. Big Sky and shoved himself into a place on the rug.

Ms. Big Sky opened the paper as best she could. In smeared pencil and squarish print, it read, "Justin Inch. My Best Frend. 2 Dogs. an A tree."

Ms. Big Sky smiled. "Thank you, Justin. That was very interesting. But is it a real story?" Her voice was impossibly tired.

"Yuh." Justin was digging dirt out of his belly button.

A little girl took his place in front of the class. With one hand, she held a crumpled piece of paper. With the other, she rolled up her skirt.

"My Mom—by Carol Peterson," she shouted.

Ms. Big Sky was from one of the seldom-mentioned states in the Midwest. She'd quit her job and moved to California because she'd inherited enough money to do so, and the weather there never dropped below forty degrees—and, she often reminded herself, she loved children. Mostly, she loved them from June 17 to August 31, when the school closed down for summer vacation.

After the readings came naptime. While the children slept, the teacher called Justin's parents. Justin's father, Clyde Inch, answered the phone.

Clyde Inch had grown up in a coal-mining town in Murray City, Ohio, that had last mined coal fifty years before Mr. Inch was born, thereby robbing Mr. Inch of the privilege of ever having worked there. When Justin was still a baby, the coal mine owners converted the old mine into a mall in a cave, the first of its kind, and named it Mine All Mine. They hoped the cool, deep shadows and mysterious ambiance would attract tourists and much-needed revenue, but no tourists came, and no one who lived in the vicinity of the nonfunctioning steel mine had money to spend foolishly, so Mine All Mine closed after only two years. The abandoned mall, formally the abandoned mine, eventually fell into itself, leaving a huge hole filled with old, moldy clothes and cheap jewelry. Mr. Inch had helped build the mall. He never quite got over his disappointment that Mine All Mine had failed. After the mall collapsed, the Inch family moved to the Bay Area in northern California. California had lots of malls, and Clyde Inch figured they could always use more.

Justin's father never felt comfortable living in the Bay Area, and the Bay Area never felt comfortable having him. His rustic, folksy nature did not fit into the cosmopolitan environment with its huge, flashy buildings and tireless bustle. So far as the Bay Area was concerned, Clyde Inch was the guy you couldn't take anywhere. The Inch family had no friends, unless you counted the neighbor next door who was always borrowing their lawnmower and forgetting to return it.

When Ms. Big Sky called Justin's house, Mr. Inch was snacking on cold pizza and a warm beer. Mr. Inch liked to keep things in balance. Had the pizza been hot, he would have wanted a cold beer. He had just separated the day's mail into two neat piles: bills stamped Overdue and bills stamped Refer to Creditor. The phone rang, and he snatched it up.

"Hello?"

A woman's voice said, "Mr. Inch?"

"Dammit, anyway. Again, you slob, you have the wrong number. I don't know any Clyde Inch. Sometimes his mail comes to this address by mistake, but I've never heard of the deadbeat. Stupid bill collectors call all the time looking for him. Call here again, I'll call the police," threatened Mr. Inch. "I've done it before, so don't think I won't!"

"I'm sorry you had to call the police, but this is not a bill collector. Is this 389-6009? I'm a teacher at Dostoevsky Elementary School calling about a student."

"Oh—excuse me; I thought you said 'Mr. Itch.' My son, Justin, goes to Does It Risky. I'm Clyde Inch, Justin's father."

"Mr. Itch, Justin read a story today that was most unusual. I would like to speak to you about it. Can you come to my classroom around four today?"

"Are you calling about Justin Inch or Justin Itch?"

"Inch, Mr. Inch. Justin *Inch*."

"I would think you'd know your students' names. It's Inch, not Itch. This is Clyde Inch, Justin Inch's father, I-n-c-h, Inch."

Ms. Big Sky was silent a moment. She tilted her head and frowned.

"Yes, I'm well aware that he's Justin Inch. If you could just come in at four, we can talk about his work."

"Yeah, OK. Me and Jus'll be there."

"Then I will see you at four, Mr. Inch."

"Yeah, sure, OK."

Mr. Inch was surprised to hear from Justin's teacher. He had never so much as looked at Justin's report cards. The Judge Junie show started at four, and he would have to miss it. He sighed and went back to his pizza. Ms. Big Sky went back to her students.

Justin got home from school around three. Mr. Inch gave him a tiny slice of pizza and sat him down.

"Justin, your teacher called me today. I'm going to your school later on to talk to her. What's going on, Jus?"

Justin was a little worried about the phone call from his teacher. He'd only ever been in trouble once, when he was five and his mother caught him in the living room peeing into the heater vent.

"Did you ever see your father do that?" she had asked angrily.

"Yes," he'd said, but she wouldn't believe him, and he hadn't felt close to her since.

Justin always told his dad the truth. His dad understood things like peeing in a heating vent out of curiosity and science fiction. He understood going where no man has gone before.

"Well, Dad, maybe the teacher called about my story. I read a story today, and all the kids liked it."

"Yeah, she said you wrote something. So what's this story about?"

"Two dogs. An' my friend who died."

"Sounds good. So, your teacher, is she pretty?"

"No, Dad."

"Dammit."

Mr. Inch glanced up at the kitchen clock. Justin used to love to look at that clock, which was brown and yellow and shaped like a dachshund. The cloud cave had no shape or colors at all—it was just soft, empty, and white.

"Let's go, Jus." Mr. Inch reached for his little boy's hand.

When they got to the school, Justin took his father to his classroom. Ms. Big Sky was waiting.

"Mr. Inch, thank you for coming in. I am Ms. Big Sky, Justin's teacher. Oh…Justin. How are you, Justin? Justin, there are some coloring books and crayons over at the art table. Why don't you go over there while I talk to your father?"

Justin gave the teacher a pissed-off look. *I can't even hear what she says about my story.* Then he thought, *Maybe it's because I'm going to get a prize.* He brightened and skipped off to the art table.

Mr. Inch seemed amused. "Your name is Big Sky?

"Yes. It's a Native American name."

"Haw, haw, haw—Big Sky—that's a good name for you. Only you're even bigger. Haw, haw, haw."

Ms. Big Sky did not invite Mr. Inch to sit down. "I'm sorry Mrs. Inch couldn't come," she said.

"She's sick," Justin's father explained. "She's mostly sick all the time, but she never complains, brave woman."

Justin's father didn't want the teacher to know that his wife worked nights delivering pizzas. By the time Justin got home from school, she was already out, and she slept in so late, he never saw her in the mornings. In fact, he saw her so rarely, she almost didn't count.

"I'm sure you're wondering why I called you, Mr. Inch," said Ms. Big Sky.

"Because that is my name?"

"I mean, I'm sure you're wondering why I called you on the telephone."

"I kinda figured it was about Justin." He spit out another laugh.

"Mr. Inch, I'm sorry to tell you this, but I suspect that Justin is a special-needs child."

"I had no idea! How wonderful. Our family isn't exactly known for being special. My wife's great-great-grandfather is the only Inch that ever made a name for himself. They hung him as a horse thief. Got a mention in a history book, even."

"Justin is a most unusual child. Does he socialize at home?"

"Naw. He's mostly alone."

"Does that worry you?"

"Justin just seems to want to lie low. I'm surprised you even know his name. Haw, haw!"

"Well, we certainly know his name. We've been very concerned about Justin."

"Say—to spend the night in a teepee, do you have to make a reservation? Haw!"

Ms. Big Sky ignored Mr. Inch's joke and continued talking.

"I've spoken with Justin many times after school. He says he wants to be part of the class, but nobody likes him. I told him not everyone can be liked. He asked me if I was talking about myself."

"Haw!" Mr. Inch was having a great time.

Justin spit on the art table. He scribbled the mess with a red crayon until it made a sticky goo. Justin hated crayons. Crayons were for decoration. They couldn't make anything. Justin looked around the room until he found one of his favorite toys, a black permanent magic marker. It was lying on the little shelf that ran along the bottom of the beautiful, blank chalkboard. The little boy stood on a chair so that he could draw a really big picture. He drew pretty well for an eight-year-old.

Justin grunted with concentration. He added some finishing touches and then stood back to take it all in. He had drawn a huge pancake face attached to a small naked body from which sprang an enormous penis.

"Look at the face—the spitting image of him," his father said proudly.

Ms. Big Sky's posture stiffened. "Perhaps an inappropriate drawing for so young a boy, especially in so public a place as a schoolroom."

"Justin could draw from the time he picked up a pencil. I wouldn't be at all surprised if he took it up one day as a job. Wouldn't surprise me at all. Me, I'm a construction worker, myself. As I said before, our family isn't exactly known for being special. My wife's great-great-grandfather, he was hung as a horse thief." People seemed to find that little detail about his wife's family history interesting.

"Mr. Inch, have you considered taking Justin to see a psychologist?"

"We're not that kind of people," Mr. Inch said sternly. "Keep your religion to yourself, Pocahontas." He grabbed Justin's hand and left.

Ms. Big Sky tried to clean the chalkboard with some damp paper towels, but the ink had already set.

As Justin and his father walked home together, they bonded over their mutual dislike for the teacher. Justin's father took his wiggly little boy's hand.

"Son, that Injun woman at the school called me, must have been three hours ago. She was that taken. Said you were special. Don't remember anything special about our family. Me, I'm just a laborer. A laborer is a guy who works his ass off until he can't anymore and then goes on disability. That lady said everyone at the school knew your name. It was your mother named you Justin. It was her great-great-grandfather's name. His last name was Le Barge, same as your mom's before she married me. This Le Barge, he was a smart guy, stole maybe a hundred horses by the time they hung him. They hung him with the whole town watching and a party after. Your mother used to cry whenever I joked around about it. She loved him because she never knew him. A relative who's a stranger is always better than a relative you know. A stranger's a lot more likely to lend you money. I can swear to that. I been there before. Nobody in my family ever lent me money, nor left me nothing neither, and I knew 'em all, excepting I didn't blame the ones what didn't have nothing to give.

"What I mean to tell you, son, is you're the first Inch that's ever measured up. Someday, someone will be reading a book, and I'll say, 'My boy wrote that. My boy is Justin Inch.'"

Justin was eight. At only eight years old, he had impressed both his teacher and his father.

Justin and his father got home just in time for their favorite program, *Good Time Monster Truck Rally.* They always watched it together, two men bonding over loud, heavy machines manned by daredevil warriors. Justin's father grabbed a beer, gave Justin a sip, and father and son settled down on the couch. Now and then, Mr. Inch would sneak a proud look at Justin. A Twinkie commercial came on, followed by one for a tampon you could wear for riding a horse. The two of them talked during the tampon commercial.

"So your story about the dogs—how did the other kids like it?"

Justin stared dully at the television. "They liked it. Jenny was rolling around, Jeff and Kelly got in a big fight, and everybody was barking. They all listened to my story, and they all said it was really, really good."

"That sounds like a great story, Jus."

"After that, Carol Peterson read her story, but nobody really liked it as much as mine and..."

"Shh. Hey, Jus, the show's starting."

Good Time Monster Truck Rally exploded onto the screen. A '91 Ford F250 pick-up chased an '85 Ram 1500 through the mud. They both got stuck and had to be pulled out by a T-35 Russian tank that ran over three Mazda CX 5s on their way to rescue the guys in the trucks.

Mr. Inch peered at the TV. "Can't even tell what truck's what, with all that mud."

More commercials. First, one for Captain Crunch and then another about a man who was popular with good-looking women because he'd had a procedure to enlarge his penis. Mr. Inch tried to distract Justin. Those sugary cereals were expensive, and Justin whined for them all the time, especially Captain Crunch.

"So, Jus, in your story, someone died?"

Justin turned from the television. "Yeah, my best friend got eaten up by two dogs. He got all ate up."

"That's fine, Justin. That's just fine."

The truck rally was on again. A fifteen-foot-high GMC Sierra known as The Grave Digger ran over four Chevy Silverados and then smashed a Dodge Ram into the wall. The tank came out again and pushed all five trucks into each other until they made a hot ball of steaming metal, which the tank promptly climbed.

Another commercial. This one was for a new-and-improved design for catheters. The next commercial advertised tomorrow's airing of *Good Time Monster Truck Rally*. The next was an attorney telling you to call his office to get money if you or a loved one had died.

"So when the dogs got your friend, you wrote about the blood and all?" Mr. Inch asked.

"Yeah. Lots of it. You couldn't even tell my best friend's face! His mom cried."

Mr. Inch slapped his knee. "Ain't that something? A real life story— you wrote a goddamned, blood-and-guts adventure story. Where is it any-way? We should put it up on the refrigerator. Hey, wait a minute. The show's on again."

Now, the tank was in the very center of the track. The monster trucks came alive and their disabled carcasses charged the tank from all sides. A massive crash exploded throughout the stands, and the crowd screamed. It ended with a Toyota Takoma wobbling away from the heap and then exploding. The show always finished with a Toys "R" Us commercial.

"That was the best damn monster truck rally I ever seen!" said Mr. Inch. "Never saw a tank before, but it sure kicks ass on a monster truck."

"Dad, there was a man named Mr. Betty, and everyone liked when I told his name—"

"Hey, Jus, someone's knocking on the door. Probably your mom with dinner."

Nearly every night, Justin's mother dropped off an unclaimed pizza for Justin and his dad. Justin and his father always ate in front of the TV on fancy TV trays made of real wood.

Justin scurried to the door. When he opened it, his mother stood there holding a cardboard pizza box on which was printed in black cursive, "Hi-Ho Pizza—and Away We Go!" She wore a red T-shirt and a baseball cap, both also printed with the Hi-Ho logo.

"Hi, Mom," Justin said.

"Hey, Jus. Gotta Hawaiian tonight. Ham and pineapple. You like pineapple, Justin?"

"Uh-huh."

She went inside and set the pizza on the table. Justin opened the pizza box, and Mr. Inch came sniffing.

"Mm—wonderful smell. I'm so hungry I could eat the kind with anchovies."

"Well, they say the way to a man's heart is through a pizza."

"Never get tired of it. Most perfect food in the world. Ever notice they never ate pizza in *The Godfather*?"

"Yes, I've always wondered about that. I mean, they spend so much time on the road, but every time it shows them eating, it's spaghetti. Pizza's a lot easier to eat on the run than spaghetti."

Mr. Inch blew on the pizza to cool it. He took a slice and bit into it. A string of cheese hung from his lip, and he hooked it back into his mouth with his tongue.

"This pizza's got pineapple on it. Who the hell puts fruit on pizza? Hey, Hon, I forgot to tell you I met Justin's teacher today. She's an injun woman—haw! Name of Ms. Big Sky."

"Her first name is Big?"

"Oughta be. No, she's one of them modern-type ladies, goes by two last names. I'm takin' the fruit off the pizza. You don't like fruit on pizza, do you, Jus?"

He turned back to his wife. "So this Big Sky lady tells me she wants to see me that same day, that afternoon, it couldn't wait. Me and Justin, we walked down to the school. Jus wrote a story that his teacher liked so much she had him read it to the class. Said our boy was special. Said the whole school knows his name. Then Jus draws one of his pictures, a real big one, of himself right there on the chalkboard, and she says it should be put up in a public place instead of just a school."

"Not one of *those* pictures?"

"Yep. *Naked* art. The real thing."

Up in his sky perch, Justin was trying to shape some of the cloud fluff into a rabbit, but it wouldn't stick. *Wonder whatever happened to Ms. Big Sky?* he thought.

Mrs. Inch's cell phone was quacking. She looked at the number and rushed out the door. "Gotta go!" she yelled. Mr. Inch and Justin carried their paper plates, heavy with pizza, to the wooden trays in front of the TV.

Clyde Inch leaned back in the ratty old couch. "Justin, except for the fruit, this pizza is great—even better, it's free. We were real lucky when your mom got that job. She's a fine woman. Wish there was something I could do for her." He stared up at the ceiling and picked his nose.

"Uh-huh," Justin answered. He was annoyed that his father was talking so much. Justin usually spent the after-dinner time alone in his room. He liked to be alone to think over everything that happened during the day.

But Mr. Inch would not shut up. "Yeah, we're mighty blessed—mighty blessed. I oughta read the Bible more. Oughta read it at all, come to think of it. Oughta take you and your mom to church. My mom and dad took me to church every damn Sunday. Bored the shit out of me. Preacher was a blind man what used to be in the army in one of them wars. We kids used to sneak up on him and holler, 'Fire in the hole!' and he'd jump all around. Say, you like this flavor pizza better than the pepperoni we had last night?"

"Uh-huh."

"Justin?"

"Uh-huh."

"Justin, are you listening to me?

"Uh-huh."

"Hey, it's time for the news."

The news led with a story about a hurricane that had flattened a trailer park in Florida. Justin snuggled up to his father, looked up into his face, and gave him a child's smile.

"Listen, Jus," said Mr. Inch. "Listen, don't forget your story tomorrow. We gotta put it on the refrigerator."

Justin's little fingers curled around his father's thumb. "Really, Dad? We really gonna put it on the refrigerator? I'll get it from Ms. Big Sky. I'll get it tomorrow."

Mr. Inch leaned forward. "Hey! Los Angeles is on fire again! Haw! Haw!"

They never did get the opportunity to display Justin's story. Ms. Big Sky had put the wadded paper into his student file, along with a description of Justin's story, and an unflattering report about Justin's father. Next to Justin's name on the top of his official school file, she wrote, in red block letters, "MAY BE HAZARDOUS TO OTHER CHILDREN." When Justin asked her for his paper back, she told him that she had lost it.

Justin's father would never know what became of his son. Mr. Inch died shortly after Justin started high school. "Dad!" Justin called down from his cloud. "Dad, it isn't worth it. It's a Time-AX, Dad. A Time-AX!"

When Justin was sixteen, Mr. Inch found a temporary job laying a parking lot for a new mall. One summer's day, as Mr. Inch leaned forward to smooth the wet cement surface, his new watch popped a spring and flew off into the cement. As he stretched over to retrieve his new watch, the steamroller rolled forward. "Ding, ding, ding!" It sounded the alarm, but too late. Mr. Inch died quickly and painfully. He wasn't supposed to be working on the new parking lot. He was supposed to be holding up a sign that read Caution—Men Laying Cement. The construction company retrieved what body parts they could and poured cement over the rest. The extra work cost the property owners more, so they argued with the cement company, and the two parties split the difference.

Justin's mother buried her husband's scanty ashes illegally in a city park under an oleander bush that also died. She told Justin, "Son, I want you to know that I loved your father in spite of his shortcomings. Promise me you won't become the ass he was."

"I won't, Mom." Justin promised. He didn't. The ass that Justin became far exceeded anyone's expectations.

Justin mopped the last of his tears with a fresh piece of cloud. *Good old Dad*, he thought. He looked at the tilted cupcake button again. Dad would have fixed it in a minute. Justin pictured his father's dirty hands—those hands told people that his dad had never been to college. Justin wouldn't go either. It was unfair. Every time he thought about it, Justin got angry.

"I'd have probably graduated Mea Go Loudly," he told himself. "With a trophy with my name on it."

CHAPTER 3

Pyramid Slave

• • •

JUSTIN FAST-FORWARDED THE VIDEO TEN years, and "What Child Is This" glided effortlessly into the section of his life he'd entitled "Pyramid Slave." Justin absently tried to roll a handful of cloud into a ball.

By the time he was eighteen, Justin was pretty much baked, a hard, bad-tasting cookie with very little sugar. After his father died, Justin began to dislike his mother. Maybe he blamed her for his father's death, maybe he was sick of pizza, but he all he could think of was getting his own place where he could have women spend the night. For that, he needed a job.

Justin had no skills except for writing stories and drawing funny pictures. Doing construction like his father was unthinkable—he was no mule—and he sure as hell wasn't going to deliver pizza. Justin wanted something more than his father, more than his mother, and more than his great-great-great-grandfather who was hung as a horse thief. He would follow his star. He would be a writer.

He sweated out an essay and went to *The San Francisco Fun Times*. When the receptionist asked whom he wanted to see, he swept by her and hurried into an office whose door read Editor. A slope-eyed man sat at an ancient desk, blotting his sweaty forehead with a stained handkerchief. Justin spoke in a low, serious voice.

"Allow me to introduce myself. I am Justin Oliver Inch, and I am here to apply for a reporter's position. This essay will verify as to my talent and ability. The cover page has my name, phone number, e-mail address, and some identifying photos of myself. I should advise you that I have many offers from several worthy publications, which confidentiality laws preclude me from naming."

Justin slapped his essay on the desk. "Enjoy," he said. Then he ran and comb through his hair and left.

Why You Want to Hire Me
By Mr. Justin Oliver Inch, Journalist, Writer, and Man of Letters

Why do you want to hire Justin Oliver Inch? Why, indeed, does anyone? There are a million answers to that question.

It's not easy to describe Justin Oliver Inch, no, not at all, although many have tried and continue to do so. Some call him a Renaissance man, some call him a man of mystery, and some call him simply...a man.

Ms. Big Sky, a professor at the prestigious Does It Risky Academy, was the first to discover Justin Oliver Inch's remarkable talent. She proclaimed the eight-year-old boy a genius, and a prestigious man in a pinstriped suit and a bow tie awarded him a gold plaque. Soon afterward, Wikipedia devoted an entire website to the remarkable boy, highlighting his many accomplishments. Sadly, they had to remove the website after only six months because demand kept causing their system to crash—but Justin was not discouraged. He went on to write his classic story, *My Best Friend.*

Publishers overlooked *My Best Friend* because the only manuscript, valued at ten million dollars, disappeared before anyone had a chance to read it. The FBI suspected it was stolen, but they never found the clever culprit, and the case remains unsolved to this day.

Justin's father, Clyde Inch, died in a monster truck rally accident and did not live to see his son become famous. His mother is still alive and owns several French restaurants in the better neighborhoods of Paris.

I, Justin Oliver Inch, am hereby applying for a job as a reporter or any job as a professional writer. If you do not have a position open, I would appreciate a referral and a letter of recommendation based upon my essay. Please note that my attorney has advised me to with-hold permission to print my essay in your newspaper at this time.

Mr. Justin Oliver Inch

Justin called *The San Francisco Fun Times* later that day, and they offered him a telemarketing job selling subscriptions to *The San Francisco Fun Times*. He went to *The East Bay Trumpet* with "Why You Want to Hire Me." They called the next day and offered him a telemarketing job selling subscriptions for *The East Bay County Trumpet*. Justin sent his essay and a short paragraph of introduction to *Snooze News*, *None of Your Business*, *Parakeet Paper*, and every California-based newspaper he could think of. All of them had job openings for telemarketers to sell subscriptions to their newspapers, but nobody wanted a reporter.

Justin wondered, *Is it possible they didn't read my essay?* He decided that it must be the case. One day, they would remember him and regret it.

Perhaps something temporary until a reporter's job comes through, Justin told himself. *But not telemarketing. Telemarketing's worse than delivering piz-zas.* For now, money was getting tight. Humiliating as it was, he went to a temporary-job agency.

The agency was in a cheap office building in one of the better parts of the worst side of town. The office door said Lucky Temp Agency. Justin walked into a dusty waiting room with a tired plastic plant. A bald man whose feet did not reach the floor sat on a couch, filling out forms. A woman at a desk behind a glass window thrust her long nose at him through a hole in the glass.

She said nothing, only waited for him to speak.

Justin guessed the woman at the front desk was around ninety years old. She was, in fact, fifty-six. Justin leaned forward and shouted, "I'm here about a job!"

The bald man looked up from his forms and stared at Justin.

"Are you hard of hearing, young man? We have special placement pro-grams for the disabled," the woman said.

Justin thought it remarkable that so old a person could still hear.

"Excuse me. I have just left a job interview at *The San Francisco Fun Times* with the editor, fine man, but stone deaf. Luckily, he was still able to read my work and was very impressed, but the boss had already promised his sister to hire her son. It's always that way, isn't it? I'm looking for work as a writer. I'm quite skilled—when I was only eight years old, a very famous instructor, Professor Big Sky, invited me to share examples of my work with a roomful of her students. In fact, I happen to have one of my essays with me. I've been discussing it with several interested parties."

"We don't have any jobs for writers. I have a permanent job for someone answering phones in our office—just opened up."

"Do I get my own desk?"

"Yes."

"And this job, it's permanent?"

"Yes."

"What is the pay?"

"Minimum wage, but you get five days unpaid vacation a year. I usually go to Reno."

Justin sighed. He would at least have his own desk.

"I'll take it."

The following day, eighteen-year-old Justin Inch was answering phones at Lucky Temp Agency. He settled in quickly. There were lots of phone calls and photocopying to do and, although it was very boring work, it kept him busy. *But I'm working in an office, at my own desk, with my own name plaque...and a writing job may come along any time,* Justin would remind himself. The days became weeks, the weeks became months, and after a year, Justin had settled in. He was living by himself now in an old, ratty apartment in an old, ratty neighborhood. He had some used furniture, a mailbox, and his own cell phone number. He got used to going to work every day, but he never got used to the other employees. They were always calling him for something.

"Justin Inch—answer the phone!"

"Justin Inch! Hey, Just—an—Inch!" Snickers from the cubicles.

Irritated, Justin answered the phone. "Hello, may I help you? You say you're out of work? Have you even tried? Do you even know what work is? What the hell is wrong with you?"

He told the next caller he had a wrong number and hung up. They called back.

"Justin Inch! Phone!"

Justin snatched up the receiver and stopped himself before he threw it against the wall.

"Yyyyyaaaaa? Ya, ya, vee haben ine jobbin, ine jobbin zere goot, goot payen. Vennen zu comen?"

Justin sensed a coworker-spy lurking around the corner and went back to his normal voice.

"Hello. This is Mr. Inch speaking. Yes, I see. I'm so sorry. Damn immigrants. That was Amadeus, our janitor. 'Amadeus, neine zee phonen! Neine!'" As Justin spoke, he repeatedly swatted the desk with a rolled up magazine. "Yes, come right down. We have lots of jobs. A janitor's position just opened up. We can probably place you today. Many of our clients find permanent work with a company they've been temping for. No...no... we've never spoken before. I'd have remembered you. You have a great voice. Are you an actor?"

The sneaky coworker stopped by. "How's it going, Justin Inch?" he asked suspiciously.

"Busy, busy as hell," Justin answered.

"Were you speaking German, Justin Inch?" the coworker asked.

"Music," Justin said. "German folk songs. Lovely stuff. The singer is usually accompanied by an accordion." Justin hummed a tuneless tune.

"See ya around, Justin Inch."

See ya around, just an asshole, Justin thought.

There were lots of different ways to joke around answering the phones. Sometimes he imitated Elvis, sometimes he played "The Star Spangled Banner" on a kazoo, sometimes he—oh, there were so many ways, and Justin enjoyed humiliating the poor suckers looking for work as much as his coworkers enjoyed humiliating him. He worked there for four years. Then, due to an economic upturn, Lucky Temp Agency went out of business. Justin was twenty-two.

CHAPTER 4

Justin is Reborn as Jollie

● ● ●

JUSTIN LEANED FORWARD OUT OF the cloud. One of the highlights of the video was when he succeeded in changing his name from Justin to Jollie. When Lucky Temp Agency went under, Justin started calling himself "Ollie" and wrote J. Ollie Inch on all his correspondence. In due time, government computers changed J. Ollie Inch to Jollie Inch. For years, Justin tried to correct the mistake by writing letters.

> Dear Ignorant Government Bum,
> My first name is J. Ollie, and my last name is Inch. Please take your head out of your back passage and correct your idiotic error.
> Yours Very Truly,
> J. Ollie Inch

Months later, he'd get an answer on expensive coated paper.

> Dear Mr. Jollie Inch: We appreciate your interest in this matter.
> Signed, §μπ∞ ¥. βπⓋⓋⓘ
> Acting Assistant Supervisor, United States Office of Counter Intelligence Proliferations

After several such responses, he decided that a Jollie Inch was preferable to a Justin Inch, and embraced the new name. *Stand back world—there's a new Inch in town*, he thought. He never used the name Justin again.

CHAPTER 5

Impressions and the WWW

● ● ●

THREE MONTHS AFTER LUCKY TEMP closed down, Justin, now Jollie had still not found work as a reporter. Rent had been due for two months, he was down to three boxes of macaroni and cheese, and still nothing. He began applying for jobs that had nothing to do with writing or art, he applied for any job that did not involve physical labor or fast food. Finally, a place called The Wonderful World of Wicker called him to interview the following day for a position as a mail clerk. The office was only three miles from his apartment.

Jollie arrived at the interview a half hour early. The place looked profitable—the offices took up an entire floor, and there were lots of cubicles with computers, a copy room, and even a water cooler you didn't have to pay for. It was a suboffice—the factory was located in Nevada, where land was cheaper and there were no corporate taxes.

He introduced himself to the receptionist. "I'm Madge," she said and handed him a job application exactly like the application he had filled out online. Jollie used his favorite writing instrument, a black marker, to fill it out.

Name—Jollie Inch
Other names—None
Criminal Record—

He'd been ticketed for jaywalking once, but jaywalking was not a real crime because everyone did it—he wrote, "None."

Three References—John F. Kennedy, Roger Wilko, Barbie Doll

Just let 'em try to find one of them!

Driver's License—Yes, I have been driving a long time now.
Social Security Number—I do well in social situations, especially those involving people. I am secure in my abilities to do so.
Prior Employment—prestigious firm, Lucky Temp Agency. Firm went out of business three months ago because owner died.

"OK," said the receptionist. "Now comes the interview. Joe! Gotta possible!"

"Excuse me, Miss Receptionist-Lady. What exactly is the nature of this establishment?" Jollie asked smoothly.

"The Wonderful World of Wicker is a wicker-basket factory. Most of the employees refer to it as WWW."

"Ah! Yes, of course. Excuse me; I've been on so many interviews lately." Jollie smiled and made a tiny bow with his head.

"Joe!" hollered the receptionist lady.

The interview lasted only a few minutes.

"Why do you want to work at the Wonderful World of Wicker?" Joe, a bored, red-eyed man asked.

Jollie ran his fingers though his hair. "I'm quite a go-getter. If you call my supervisors at Lucky Temp, they'll tell you the same—that is they'd tell you if the owner hadn't died or if I knew where the other employees were. I know I'll be a big asset to the company—and I love wicker."

"Sounds OK. It isn't exactly a genius position. I guess you can handle it," Joe said.

Jollie was pleased the interview had gone so well. Perhaps they'd heard of him from Lucky Temp before it'd gone out of business. Damn, he'd been good. He was probably the best damn phone answerer Lucky Temp had ever had, and he'd rock this job too.

Lunchtime at WWW was at 11:30. From his cloud, Jollie watched himself toss the mail aside and go into the employee lunchroom.

Seven bored employees sat at a rectangular table in a faded room. There was an old microwave and a rancid refrigerator nobody cleaned—that unpleasant task was called "somebody else's job." A trashcan filled with smelly paper bags, sticky soda cans, and unwanted food over-flowed. Now, swollen by a successful employment history, Jollie took advantage of every opportunity to talk about his achievements. He usually spent his lunch hour giving motivational speeches to his fellow employees from a makeshift podium made from a stack of old phone books.

His most recent theme was "Impressions."

"The topic today is impressions—let me repeat—*impressions.* The dictionary defines an impression as 'an imitation of a person or sound, done for entertainment.' What impression do you make? An uncomfortable question, isn't it? I can see most of you squirming right now. But what is the value of an impression? Is it really important? Let us not kid ourselves, gentlemen—oh, and you women too.

"Step one—never be afraid to lie. The Bible teaches us, 'To thine own self be true.' Sounds nice, doesn't it? Bullshit. Nobody ever achieved anything by being thine own self. If a man is to prosper, he must be somebody better than himself. In short, he must make a formidable impression, no matter how dismal his beginnings, no matter how great the lie. Never be afraid to lie—I never was, and look where it's gotten me.

"The next step is to dress in proper clothes. A man in fine clothes, even a moron, can be anything, regardless of his failings. In my power-red Hermes tie and Penney's sports coat, I am that man. When I walk into a room, you see me, and I see you. We have not met, but I have already impressed you. There are not many men in the world who own a Hermes tie, you can be sure of that!

"The third step is to abandon all friends and family and mix wholly with strangers who are unaware of your insignificant status. Because you are a stranger, you can be anything you want—a postman, a barman, even a fireman. But before you chose what to be, immediately ask whoever you're meeting what his profession is. Then make yours is something that threatens his. For example, someone might tell me, 'I'm a politician,' and I might say, 'I'm an honest news reporter.'

"The fourth step is to always treat people as inferiors, especially in the company of others. Sarcasm and irrefutable insults minimize a man and elevate the person who subjects that man to entertaining public ridicule. For example, I might say, 'Hey, Bernard, is your wife sober yet?'"

Bernard Sledge called out, "My wife is neither sober nor a drunk! She has a drinking *problem*. And that fancy tie you're always talking about came from the Big Cheese's office, and you know it!"

"Are you doubting my veracity?" asked Jollie.

"I'm calling you a liar!" Bernard answered. "And a thief! Yes, I'm calling you a common, low-down thief!"

"Hold on, hold on," said Charlotte, the office peacekeeper. "Now, let's be fair. We don't have any evidence that Jollie took the Hermes tie, even though we all know he stole it during the fire drill. But even a liar and a thief has the right to a fair trial. The important thing to remember is that here in the United States a person is innocent until proven guilty. Oh—also, we shouldn't call Bernard's wife a drunk, either without absolute proof."

Nick Smith enthusiastically agreed. "Hear, hear! Neither a liar, a drunk nor a thief! God bless America!"

Big Bart stood up and addressed Bernard. "So, you don't like America? So get the hell out! I fought for this country—I fought!" The huge man leaned forward and lowered his forehead like a bull ready to charge.

Lou, who was even bigger than Big Bart, now stood up. "You're not welcome in this lunchroom," he told Bernard. Bernard weighed only one hundred and thirty pounds and was sixty years old. He got the hell out.

Lou walked over and shook Jollie's hand. "Thank you, Jollie. Thank you for standing up for America."

Jollie always felt proud when Lou shook his hand in the video. "Ah, Big Lou—I kind of miss the guy," he murmured, and sniffed into a handful of cloud.

None of his coworkers had ever seen Jollie wear the Hermes tie. Jollie kept the brilliant red tie carefully wrapped in white tissue paper in a box on a shelf of his closet at home. He'd filched it only last month from his boss's office. They'd had a fire drill, and Jollie had lingered behind and taken it from the coat rack. He'd never worn it anywhere, but sometimes he put it on and walked around his apartment, greeting invisible people in a deep voice and shaking invisible hands. *And the boss never missed it, never even mentioned it was gone*, he'd remind himself whenever he looked at it.

Jollie was fired anyway. He hadn't been proven guilty and was, there-fore innocent, but everyone knew he'd stolen the tie. Melody Justice had seen him running down the stairwell with it swinging from the back of his pants on the morning of the fire drill. She told everyone, but no one ever said anything to the higher-ups, because the lower-downs all hated the bosses more than they did one another.

Jollie didn't think of himself as thief—he didn't steal; he looked for opportunities. If he found a wallet, he would keep the money and throw the wallet away. He ate unpaid-for fruit in the grocery store. He took towels, sheets, hangers, and robes from hotels. No big deal. Not a thief but a man who made the most of his opportunities.

The day he was fired, his coworkers held a going-away party in the dusty gray lunchroom. Jollie made a speech.

"I want to thank you all for this grand affair. I suppose I know more about wicker than anyone. Many of you know that a lynch mob hung my great-great-great-grandfather for stealing horses, but I mean to elevate the name Inch. I have always been considered special, as many of you can at-test. I had a teacher once, Ms. Big Sky, who couldn't stop talking about me."

WWW fired him just six months shy of his working there for nine years. Jollie loved the part where they brought out the Secureway cake. "It even had my name on it—in pink icing," he would say and happily sigh.

His coworkers sang "For He's a Jolly Good Fellow," ate the cake, and quickly forgot about him.

The going-away party blurred. Jollie sped the video up a year to the part where he had, at last, discovered a way to showcase his talent. Jollie was still not working. At only thirty years old, he'd already held two jobs and made quite a name for himself. How remarkable that a man with his gifts should be out of work! It was just a matter of time before he found something. The unemployment checks helped. Meanwhile, he would hone his skills until they were razor-sharp. His future was just around the corner.

CHAPTER 6

Opportunity

● ● ●

JOLLIE'S MOUTH WATERED AS HE watched himself cooking an Inch family favorite, Top Ramen and chili. It was an automatic response—he hadn't felt hungry since he'd died. The familiarity of his apartment's beat-up furniture and ratty futon comforted him.

The bedroom, which was also his living room, butted up against a tiny bathroom, resplendent with twisted and mildewed towels, a cracked soap dish, and a big-screen television mounted on the wall across from the toilet. He sat there now, reading from an adult-school catalogue.

"Boy, do I miss my bathroom," said Jollie.

He hunched forward, squinting at the tiny print of the catalog, concentrating on the lists of classes scheduled for the next session. After reading through them, then through them again, after perusing the registration procedures and the semester's many options, Jollie stood up and flushed the toilet.

His eyes flashed excitement. *A Creative Writing Class...Creative. Just the thing—a perfect fit. Dry newspaper stories about town meetings and church charities—what was I thinking? Here's something exciting and dramatic, something that will have people asking one another, 'Have you heard? Where have you been? Jollie Inch has a new book! The whole world is calling him the world's greatest writer.*

Jollie set the catalog reverently down on the TV tray that served as a table. He woke up three times that night to pee.

The next morning was Friday—a crisp, cool Friday in early January, his favorite month of the year. He liked the naked birch trees that shivered in the fog, liked their discomfort and how the wind swept away the past in preparation for a future that might be worse. Anything could happen in January. It was the first of twelve months of change.

Class started in two days, on the twelfth. It was three months long, long enough, Jollie thought, to prove to everyone just who he was. Jollie felt uplifted, excited by the prospect—surely this—surely *this*—was everything he had waited for. It was what Ms. Big Sky had seen in him, what his father had praised. It slept inside him, ready to explode. A year ago, he would have been getting ready for work. That was all over now.

Jollie skipped coffee and set out that morning for Millard Fillmore Elementary-Adult Education. He hadn't been outside for days, and the sparkling yellow sun stabbed at his eyes. A freezing breeze pushed him toward the car, and he quickened his step to stop the cold ache in his feet.

As Jollie drove his old Chevy to the school, he hummed along to the engine's clickety-clack sound. The dull, rectangular buildings of Millard Fillmore squatted behind a wall of fast-food restaurants whose drive-through speakers never ceased announcing food orders. A graveyard parking lot glazed over with unmolested ice indicated that classes hadn't started yet. Jollie parked and walked through the gate into the school. He followed an arrow on a helpful sign that read, "Adult School Education Office This Way—Questions Received Cheerfully, Answers Given Cautiously."

The office smelled like new paint and old hamburgers. A woman missing a tooth spoke to Jollie from behind a huge wooden desk that eclipsed her tiny frame. "May I help you?" she asked in a flat voice.

"Yes, my good lady. Yes, you may. I am here to sign up for the creative writing class. My secretary called yesterday and made an appointment. My name is Jollie Inch. Mr. Jollie Inch."

"Most of our students register online. In fact, all of them do. I haven't had a student come into the office to register in years."

Jollie shifted from foot to foot.

"Do you need to use the restroom?" the woman asked Jollie.

"No, no, indeed. As I said, I am here, good lady, to register for the creative writing class. It is imperative that I get in. Should the class be full, I am sure the instructor will make an exception in my case. You see, I am one of those rare people who were meant to write. To write, you understand. To change lives with words."

"Congratulations—here are some forms for you to read and fill out. I can help you with that."

"Thank you, my good lady, I already know how to read," Jollie said. "I've been reading since I was five years old. At eight, I wrote a prize-winning piece of *nonfiction*, that means true, that my teacher, Ms. Big Sky, brought to the attention of the school principal. It amazed everyone who read it. Unfortunately, the original document was stolen before it could be published."

Jollie filled out the forms and hurried out. "Good day, good lady. One day, you will say, 'I knew him—I knew Jollie Inch.' I may not remember you—fame brings many admirers—but I thank you for your future gratitude."

The good lady took the papers and threw them into an overflowing box.

Jollie almost skipped back to his car. What luck! He thought. He had avoided the crowds of students enrolling, and probably guaranteed himself a spot in the creative writing class. His only regret was that his talents would be wasted in a cheap adult-education class rather than celebrated at a prestigious university with a high price tag. Jollie spent the next two days on an essay that was sure to win him wild applause, applause that would be much, much louder than the children's insignificant smattering that day in Ms. Big Sky's class when he was eight years old.

The creative writing class met three times a week from five to seven in the evening. The school was named for Millard Fillmore, the thirteenth president of the United States, but so few people knew who Millard Fillmore was that the city had affixed a plaque on the wall in front of the school that read, "Our School Is Proudly Named for Millard Fillmore, the Unsung President."

The first evening of class, Jollie had to wipe his sweaty hands on his pants to turn the overheated Chevy into a parking space. He exited the car, walked toward the gates of the school, remembered he had forgotten his bag with its notebooks and pens, returned to the car, panicked when he saw his bag was not there, remembered he had put his bag in the trunk, opened the trunk, retrieved his bag, and again walked toward the school. As he passed the gates, he noticed the plaque honoring President Millard Fillmore.

President of what? Jollie asked himself when he read the sign—and then gave it no more thought. He couldn't be bothered with some unsung president of a small-town elementary-adult school. He had his future to plan.

His thoughts were spinning creativity.

My being there will be like Jesus Christ eating his last supper at a Kentucky Fried Chicken. It will be like Mikhail Baryshnikov dancing the hokey-pokey. It will be like Winston Churchill leading a Boy Scout meeting.

Jollie chuckled over his own cleverness. When he found the classroom, he waited on the side of the building, where he could watch the other students go in. He waited until they were all inside and the teacher closed the door. Then he went in. Jollie gave the teacher, Jud Roy Lebowitz, a quick nod and sat down in the back, where he could both hide from and observe the other students.

CHAPTER 7

Professor Jud Roy Lebowitz

● ● ●

"So, let's take a look at the famous professor," sneered Jollie from his cloud. After all these years, he still hated him.

Jud Roy Lebowitz was born Jud Roy Higgle, but as soon as they heard his name, people treated him like he was stupid, and by the time he was in college, he was damned sick of comments about killer moonshine, inbred children, and possum stew. He was damned sick of it, and although for the Higgle family—formally of Spittoon Spat, Tennessee—such things were commonplace, Jud Roy wanted better. A used car dealer who had given him his first job discovered that the nineteen-year-old had a talent for selling cars that languished in a lot salesmen referred to as Dead on Arrival. Selling cars paid for college and cheating on exams kept him in college long enough to graduate with a BA in English. The day after he graduated, Jud Roy Higgle paid an attorney to change Higgle to Lebowitz. He chose the name Lebowitz because it was Jewish, and Jews had a reputation for doing well in school and for becoming rich and successful. They never drank to excess, always had pocket money, and came from respectable, well-dressed families. The world never expected anything from Jud Roy Higgle, but they anticipated marvels from Jud Roy Lebowitz.

When Jud Roy changed his name from Higgle to Lebowitz, he cut all ties with his family. They were neither educated nor well off, and they never understood the disadvantages of having a hick southern name. His father, Leroy Ray Higgle, had struggled for years floating from job to job.

His mother, Rhonda Louise Higgle, never worked. The best the family had ever achieved was middle-lower-class status. His parents drank a lot and hardly noticed when Jud Roy stopped coming around.

Now and then, he'd run into someone named Lebowitz who asked about his name. "Someone told me that your last name is Lebowitz—I'm Henky Lebowitz from Long Island, son of Mildred and Jacob Lebowitz. Do you come from the East Coast? Maybe we're related."

Whenever this happened, he would take a relaxed, bored attitude and say, "Nice to meet you, Henky. I'm Jud Roy Lebowitz—yes, Lebowitz is my last name. I don't know if we have relatives in Long Island. Perhaps you know my father, Dr. Harvey Lebowitz. He's a gynecologist at the Harry Nevus Medical Center on the Isle of Man. Or last I heard, he was there—it's been a while—" and here, Jud Roy would lower his eyes. "Fine, he's fine, just—well, I don't like to say."

Henky Lebowitz would frown. "I'm not sure I know of a Harvey—oh, yes, yes, I may—he's Janet's son. My great-aunt, Janet Lebowitz, her son's a gynecologist somewhere overseas. When you see your father, when you see Harvey, tell him you talked to Dr. Henky Lebowitz—we may have worked together at Yale New Haven. Your father's aunt was my wife's grandmother. Her husband was Dr. Mort Sedman. What do you do, Jud Roy? A physician like your father?"

"I also planned on becoming a gynecologist, but father advised against it. He always told me, 'Jud—Jud, go your own way. Don't let anyone interfere with your goals. Just remember never to ask a dumb question—it's not good for business.'"

"Very true. Harvey was always smart that way—he kept two sets of books, as I recall. You could do no better than to follow his advice," Henky would say.

Jud would continue. "Yes, my father is still as smart as—well, I mean, as can be expected. I don't like to say. Anyway, I followed his advice and made my own way. I mean to go into advertising after I finish my doctorate in *Les Belles de Escriber* in Paris. Modesty aside, I have a talent for selling things. I've written several television commercials, mostly in France, although I would consider a position with an agency here in the United States."

The next day, Dr. Henky Lebowitz would tell his sister, Dr. Sara Feinstein, under the strictest of confidence, about Jud Roy's father, Dr. Harvey Lebowitz. Dr. Sara Feinstein would tell her husband, Dr. Myron Feinstein, who would promise to say nothing but instead call his cousin Gershom's father, Dr. Shemp Lebowitz, for more information. After hearing what had happened, Dr. Shemp Lebowitz would call his friend, Dr. Jonathan Goldfarb, who would swear to keep the whole matter to himself but instead tell his mother, Dr. Linda Goldfarb, who would promise to say nothing, but she never could keep a secret, so soon everybody knew. They would all want to help poor Harvey, whom nobody had heard from for the longest time, and they would continually call one another so their conversations resounded in a chorus of concern.

Jud Roy began receiving invitations to Saturday dinners with lots of singing and handholding. He always wrote a thank-you note. Jud Roy's new family connections landed him a job as a technical writer at Johnson Y Johnson's. He was only twenty-three years old. His starting salary topped what his father would ever make.

The truth was that, although grammatically correct, Jud Roy's writing was diligent, boring, and just passable enough to enable him to keep his job. After six years, Johnson Y Johnson's let him go. Jud Roy's Jewish family admired him for leaving Johnson Y Johnson's to look for something more challenging—but Jud Roy had no savings, having frittered his salary away on whiskey and women, and he needed work badly. Rent was due, he hadn't paid his bar tab in—*how long?*—and if he didn't take care of those parking tickets, dammit, he'd lose his license again. He found lots of jobs for which he was not qualified—forms auditor, paperwork processer, welder, stevedore—until finally—*here's one that sounds good. Creative Writing Teacher at Millard Fillmore Elementary-Adult Education.* The hours were short and the money just enough.

CHAPTER 8

Superintendent Bob Bottomly

● ● ●

JUD ROY SENT THE NECESSARY applications to the Oakland City School District, and a week later, a polite voice called from the school district office asking if he was still interested in the job. Jud Roy gave an enthusiastic yes, and the voice scheduled an interview with the school superintendent, Mr. Bob Bottomly.

As soon as the polite voice hung up, Jud Roy searched the Internet for Bob Bottomly's name. The only hit was the following:

> In June of nineteen seventy-eight, the city of Oakland, California, built an elementary school and named it after Millard Fillmore, the thirteenth president of the United States. Robert James Bottomly, a city council member, made a substantial contribution to the school on the stipulation that it be named for President Millard Fillmore, whom Robert Bottomly claimed was a distant relative on his grandmother's side. Millard Fillmore was president from 1850 to 1853 and is best known for enacting new bankruptcy laws eliminating debtor's prison.

"Here comes the eye guy," Jollie remarked. He sneezed from a bit of cloud fluff that floated in the air.

Superintendent Bob Bottomly's office was neat as a pin and almost empty of books and papers. It was as though nobody ever worked there. A single blank piece of paper lay in the center of his desk.

Bob Bottomly always interviewed prospective new teachers. Jud Roy Lebowitz's interview was at four o'clock, and he arrived five minutes early. When he knocked on Mr. Bottomly's door, the superintendent jumped.

"Just a moment, please—I'll be there in—" Mr. Bottomly looked at his watch—"four and a half minutes!"

He expected people to arrive at exactly the appointed time, and he called anything else "barging in whenever they felt like it." It interfered with the celebrity judge shows he faithfully recorded every day and watched at his leisure. Reluctantly, Mr. Bottomly shut off the television and waited the remaining four and a half minutes. When his watch said four o'clock, he stood up, opened the door, and made a little bow to Jud Roy Lebowitz. Mr. Bottomly always spoke in a deep, manly rumble that stressed his throat.

"Good morning, sir. You must be Professor Lebowitz. My, my—what an interesting coat. One rarely sees a red plaid sport coat. Please come in, Professor." Jud Roy did so.

Jud Roy stepped forward to shake Mr. Bottomly's hand, which was pinkishly clean. The superintendent declined. "I never touch a man's hand," he explained. "I am very conservative." Jud Roy stepped back.

"Glad to meet you, Mr. Superintendent. As you know, I am here to interview for the creative writing teacher's position. I last worked at Johnson Y Johnson's as a technical writer."

"And I am very glad to meet you, Professor Lebowitz. Please, sit down. Lebowitz is a Jewish name, if I remember right," said Mr. Bottomly. "Well, well, no matter. Times change…not always for the best, but not always for the worst either. Ha ha! A little joke, that's all, Professor Lebowitz. I hope you aren't offended. I'm quite a cutup, you see. Ha!" He choked on his bit of laughter and cleared his throat. "Haaa-rrrump!"

"Again, please sit down. I've already asked you once—are you hard of hearing, Professor Lebowitz?" Mr. Bottomly waited for Jud Roy to take a seat. "Comfortable?" the superintendent asked. Mr. Bottomly could not help but notice that Jud Roy slumped slightly in the chair.

The superintendent had a wandering eye that intermittently bounced in different directions like a moving target. It unnerved people. They would shift back and forth and bob their heads up and down, chasing down the skittish eye. Jud Roy shifted his head to the right, and Mr. Bottomly shifted his head to the left. Both men struggled to match the direction of the other man's eyes, and it made communication difficult.

"I have your résumé, Professor Lebowitz. It says you worked for Johnson Y Johnson's. In-ter-est-ing—very." Mr. Bottomly yawned and looked at the single paper on his desk. "Johnson Y Johnson's is a good outfit—dependable and well organized. Their commercials reflect strong family values, something one rarely sees nowadays. Such an unusual sport coat. Do you own a suit, Professor Lebowitz?"

"No, I don't, but I am not adverse to suits, so long as they are conservative."

"Ah!" said Mr. Bottomly. "Conservative—that is an excellent attitude for a professor at Millard Fillmore Elementary-Adult Education."

"Thank you, Superintendent Bottomly. I worked at Johnson Y Johnson's for six years. All my friends thought it was a very big deal that I worked there, but they did not know the amount of stress and travel expected of a top company executive. Johnson Y Johnson's is such a huge outfit, and their standards are exceedingly high. They awarded me with a bonus for some very important work I did for a top-of-the-line baby shampoo. I received the bonus for inserting 'check water temperature and rinse' into the existing instructions, thus saving countless babies from being seriously burned."

Mr. Bottomly was impressed. "I am indeed, sir, exceedingly surprised that you would leave such a grand position, I mean *situation*, as the word is. Yes, I believe situation *would* be the correct word. Indeed, I am surprised that you would leave such a grand situation. What were the circumstances of your being discharged?"

"I left voluntarily because the job did not challenge me."

"Indeed?" said Mr. Bottomly.

"Oh, yes. Yes, indeed," said Jud Roy.

Mr. Bottomly drummed his fingers on the desk. "That you seek challenge is commendable—a man should be challenged. Women, not so much. It worries them. Haaa-rrrump!" He cleared his throat again.

"Oh, yes. I am quite in agreement," Jud Roy assured him.

The job had challenged him plenty, but Jud Roy had been too lazy to keep up with Johnson Y Johnson's increasingly complex cosmetics line, so he had looked for ever-simpler products to write about. The company let him go after he submitted a set of instructions on how to use soap.

"I wouldn't bother using us as a recommendation," his boss had advised. "Good luck to you, Mr. Lebowitz."

Mr. Bottomly laid back in his chair and stared at the ceiling in a seeming trance. It helped to relax his eye but it never lasted very long. His eye suddenly jumped, and he jumped too, and then sat up quickly and leaned into Jud Roy's face. "Any military experience?"

"No—but I had a very strict father. He insisted on my making perfect grades."

Mr. Bottomly again stared up at the ceiling. "Hm—strict father. I thought so." He remained that way for a good ten minutes. Jud Roy shifted. The length of time the superintendent was taking to decide whether to hire him was becoming weird.

"Superintendent Bottomly?" Jud Roy said.

Mr. Bottomly looked down from the ceiling. "I, myself, enlisted in the navy in the nineteen hundreds—no war at the time, but it was no picnic, I assure you. Due to a prior injury, I spent most of the time answering the phone for the admiral. It was ring, ring, ring, all the time, and I answered the call. Ha! You see, I do love a little joke. After three years, they allowed that I man a telescope. For that assignment, I was paid hazard—yes, I said hazard duty and received an honorable discharge."

"Ha ha," said Jud Roy. "Answered the call—you certainly are a cutup, Mr. Bottomly. One might say you were the admiral's callboy. Instead of call girl, you see. Ha!"

Mr. Bottomly did not join in with Jud Roy's laughter. "You will address me as Superintendent Bottomly," he said in a flat voice. "Also, although a superior may share a little joke with a subordinate, it is inappropriate for a subordinate to tell jokes to his superior."

"Excuse me, Superintendent Bottomly. I was swayed by your wit and forgot myself," said Jud Roy meekly.

Mr. Bottomly studied the professor's face. Jud Roy tried to dodge the wandering eye.

"Let us focus on the matter at hand, Professor Lebowitz. Sir, I have to say, indeed, I really feel that…Professor, the way I see things is that you are first and foremost a writer of *words*."

"I am proud to claim that moniker," answered Jud Roy.

"Indeed. Pride behooves a man. Professor, I am of the opinion that what we expect of a teacher here at Millard Fillmore is at the very minimum, Professor Lebowitz, *al le petit minimal*, as say the French, who shamed themselves in the Great War, that what we expect here is far beyond the usual base standards of an adult-education program. Although Millard Fillmore Elementary-Adult Education may not be Johnson Y Johnson's, our expectations are also exceedingly high. I might add that the children who attend Millard Fillmore are required to wear uniforms. We are still debating the policy for our adult students."

"I may go out and get that suit today—if it is conservative," said Jud Roy. He accidently intercepted Mr. Bottomly's eye and both men reddened and looked away. Mr. Bottomly readjusted himself in his chair.

"Ah-hem! Indeed, Mr., um, Professor Lebowitz—with regard to education, its function, as I perceive it, its purpose is learning. Knowledge, sir, is our great country's greatest weapon—more than any submachine gun, Howitzer, AK-47, or any other killing machine. Knowledge is man's crowning glory; it is the heart of…the heart of our very, of our very…"

Jud Roy finished his sentence for him. "Of our very beingness."

"Exactly! That is precisely the point I was trying to make. We begin to understand one another," said Mr. Bottomly.

"I get your point," said Jud Roy. "Do I get the job?"

"Another joke, Professor Lebowitz?"

"No indeed, Superintendent Bottomly."

A respectable time had passed for the superintendent to decide to hire Jud Roy, which was exactly what Mr. Bottomly had planned to do all along.

The supervisor stood up. "I welcome you, sir. I welcome you to Millard Fillmore Elementary-Adult Education. We run a tight ship, and we're glad to have you aboard. Ha!" A snort mixed in with his laugh.

Jud Roy stood and leaned forward to shake Mr. Bottomly's hand, remembered, and sat back down.

Then Mr. Bottomly spent a long time going over the responsibilities of the job. He finished by saying, "You will find that teaching at Millard Fillmore is a hugely rewarding experience, indeed, I would say *exceedingly* rewarding, yes, very, very rewarding indeed. Enthusiastic students will want to discuss their work after class. They may call you at home or drop by your house to seek guidance. Some will submit—unassigned, mind you—I say *unassigned* work for you to review and comment on. You will be their *instructor* in every sense of the word. The knowledge you impart will excite their minds, tickle their fancies, especially the ladies—and here, he winked his crooked, wet eye— "yes, especially the ladies. You will know the glory of being needed by truly desperate people. When I say desperate people, mind you, I mean people who *hunger*, yes, people who starve for knowledge. However, a class must have a minimum of ten students. No fewer than ten. A class with less than ten is automatically canceled. The teacher, of course, is not compensated."

Finally, Mr. Bottomly stopped talking. The only thing Jud Roy remembered was "However, a class must have a minimum of ten students. A class with less than ten is automatically canceled. The teacher, of course, is not compensated."

"Thank you, Superintendent Bottomly. I look forward to the coming semester." Jud Roy got the hell out of there.

Mr. Bottomly switched the judge show back on. "Ha ha!" he laughed. The judge had just leapt from the bench and was strangling a snotty eighteen-year-old drifter who refused to pay rent.

Jud Roy Lebowitz was a rotten teacher. Although he taught creative writing at Millard Fillmore for two years, Jud Roy himself had never actually written anything creative. He never collected the papers the students wrote, never gave advice, and did not allow questions. His teaching style made his job very easy. Thus far, Jud Roy Lebowitz had managed to reach the magical number of ten by posting flyers showing a retouched photo of himself wearing glasses he didn't need and autographing an impressively heavy hard copy of *Moby Dick* book. Beneath the photo, the flyer read:

Creative Writing Class—*Can You Meet the Challenge?*
Instructor: Professor Jud Roy Lebowitz
Jud Roy Lebowitz *is a professional writer whose work can be found in households all over the world. His short story, 'The Baby Shampoo' netted prestigious awards that resulted in monetary gain.*
Mondays, Wednesdays, and Fridays, 5:00 p.m.
to 7:00 p.m., 01/12/2015 to 04/24/2015
Millard Fillmore Elementary-Adult Education,
1234 Happy Road Ave., Oakland, California

The photograph on the poster showed that Jud Roy wasn't altogether bad looking. He was tall, dark, and slender. He had a face that people said looked like either a horse or a clown, but in a nice way. His foxlike eyes and very fair skin gave him a cold, flinty look that women found sexy, and his hair curled and frizzled so much, it never looked the same way twice. Jud Roy was single but could not afford to date.

Jollie leaned out the cloud window, tossing confetti pieces of cloud out into space.

Creative writing classes always net a few bizarre and interesting people. The semester Jollie joined the class, Jud Roy's posters did very well—he had six students more than the required ten. Out of sixteen, the class had four very strange students, making it exactly 25 percent weird, slightly above average. The four very strange students were Leslie Tomatiny, Peppy Zipline, Dino Quiet Room, and of course Jollie Inch. On the first day of class, Jud Roy always asked his students to write a paper about why they had enrolled in the class. All of the students, except for the four weird ones, wrote that they were there to "find themselves." The four weirdos wrote that they were there for "professional reasons."

CHAPTER 9

Leslie Tomatiny

● ● ●

"HEY, LESLIE!" JOLLIE HOLLERED FROM the cloud when the diminutive young woman made her appearance.

Like her mother's second husband, Leslie had blond hair and blue eyes, which was odd because Leslie's father, her mother's first husband, was a dark-eyed Italian and Leslie's mother was a Mexican beauty with coal-black hair. Being bright, Leslie could name her father and all four of her stepfathers and give a brief description of each. Her father, Mario, was loud and gross, and he chewed and talked at the same time. Rick was a surfer who got up early every day and didn't get home until late at night, if he got home at all. Her second stepfather, Larry, slept around and was arrested twice for removing his clothes in an adults-only movie theatre. The third, Kyle, never spoke or moved from the couch. Her current stepfather, Zack, smoked and chewed tobacco. He pretended to be sick all the time and expected Leslie and her mother to wait on him.

These men drifted in and out of her life, leaving only the pale shadow of an unpleasant memory. Her mother drank multiple-malt scotch and forgot a lot of important stuff, like closing the freezer door so the food wouldn't thaw out and make a smelly, drippy mess for Leslie to clean.

In keeping with children's tendency to make choices their parents do not, Leslie read books. She would only read nonfiction and enjoyed such classics as *Webster's Dictionary*, *The Encyclopedia Britannica*, and her favorite,

Euclid's Elements of Geometry. Her reading choices made her knowledgeable and boring.

When she needed to escape the ever-running television set, Leslie took long walks alone. She always pretended she had a destination. Her favorite stop was Ye Olde Grocery, an upscale, privately owned grocery store just a few miles from her house. Leslie liked the store's charming simplicity and unhurried atmosphere. She especially loved the fruit displays. She loved their dewdrop cleanliness, the neat stacks, and the duplications of shapes and colors. Sometimes, customers disrupted the perfection of the displays by moving the fruit to places it didn't belong. One morning, a woman put a Bosc pear in with the Granny Smith apples. The usually quiet Leslie angrily blocked the woman's grocery cart and faced her down.

"Ma'am, I noticed that you filed a Bosc pear in the Granny Smith apple section. Pears and apples are different fruits. Apples are round with crisp flesh. Pears are elongated and less tolerant of cold weather. *Less* tolerant, ma'am. If you leave that pear there, the warmer carbon dioxide of the apples will cause it to ripen too soon, and the pear will get brown mushy spots, which could spread to other fruit, causing spoilage."

The woman hurried away. Leslie gently returned the pear to the safety of the other Boscs.

"There, there, my dear," she said, and patted the frightened pear.

As she comforted the pear, Leslie noticed that its smooth curves and triangular shape seemed made for stacking. She began rearranging the pears into walls that became triangles that became the subject of a photograph she remembered from a *National Geographic* magazine. Four hours later, she stood back and assessed the impressive skyline of the Pyramids of Giza constructed from two hundred and eighty-three Bosc pears. Shoppers gathered around.

A woman gushed, "It's a miracle. An absolute miracle, that. As pretty as anything the Egyptians ever built."

A man spoke with authority. "Remarkable placement and balance. That structure could survive an earthquake. Notice how the bottoms of the pears dovetail into the tops. I'm an engineer, so I should know. Yes, I'm an engineer." He looked around for someone to comment on his expertise.

A woman who had traveled to Egypt stated, "I have traveled to Egypt. The Great Pyramid is, in reality, larger than depicted here. Archeologists believe that the hieroglyphics inside the Great Pyramid translate to either accounting expenditures or the pharaohs' sexual feats."

The engineer backed her up. "Yes, indeed, that's true. I know it's true."

Larger Billie, so called because he was larger than his father, Large Billie, came out of his office to see what the commotion was. Larger Billie had inherited the grocery store from his father ten years ago, and he knew the grocery store business better than anybody. Larger Billie recognized a good business opportunity when he saw it.

"That's our new produce manager," he announced to the crowd. "Hired her just today." Leslie wasn't used to the attention. She smiled crookedly and stepped on an errant grape.

A reporter and a photographer from *The Local Gazette* showed up. When the reporter interviewed a terrified Leslie, she tried to be amusing.

"Always did love triangles," she mumbled through her hair. "For a square deal, come to Ye Olde Grocery."

It was nerves, mostly. The story ran the following morning:

Ye Olde Grocery Surprises All of Livermore

There's a new attraction in the famously boring city of Livermore. Leslie Tomatiny, an employee of longtime grocery store, Ye Olde Grocery, on Main Street, has made a fruit display that rivals anything in the professional art world. She has reconstructed the skyline of the famous Pyramids of Giza, entirely of pears. When asked what inspired her bold, revolutionary display, Leslie evoked hysteria from the crowd of admirers by saying, "Always did love triangles. For a square deal, come to Ye Olde Grocery."

The photographer took a photograph of her and Larger Billie in front of the pyramid structure with Larger Billie's arm around her. The paper printed the story and the photo next day. The caption beneath the photo read, "Leslie Tomatiny Erects Fruit," and the article quadrupled the store's customer base.

Leslie continued to build fruit displays that were quite remarkable. *The Local Gazette* ran stories with photographs on two other creations, *Winged Victory* made from Bing cherries and *Hoover Dam*, from new potatoes. She carried copies of the articles and pictures of her masterpieces everywhere she went. People all over the Bay Area began talking about "grocery-store art."

"Leslie was somewhat artistic—I guess," Jollie said from his cloud.

It was a sunny afternoon, and Leslie was placing the final touches on a display she'd entitled *Zucchini on Parade*, when Carlotta Fineworth, the curator of Livermore Museum Now Open, approached her.

Carlotta's cart overflowed with economy-sized packages of day-old cookies that had been marked down, bent cans of soda that had been marked down, postseason Christmas candy that had been—her cart was filled with groceries that had been marked down.

"Excuse me, are you Ms. Leslie Tomatiny?" Ms. Fineworth asked.

"Why, yes I am," a surprised Leslie said.

Carlotta offered her hand. "So nice to meet you, Ms. Tomatiny. I am Ms. Carlotta Fineworth, the curator of the Livermore Museum Now Open, often referred to as the LMNO. Have you visited our museum, Ms. Tomatiny?"

Leslie gently took the cold, thin-skinned hand and dropped it. "Yes, ma'am. I've been to the LMNO many times. Such an interesting name."

Ms. Fineworth tightened her lips. "The name, of course, was supposed to be Livermore Museum. Mr. Whitehill, the old fool, ordered the permanent sign, but he told the sign company to put Livermore Museum Now Open, which was supposed to be for a paper banner announcing the museum's opening. That stupid sign cost the city fifty thousand dollars! We couldn't afford to have a new one made."

Leslie nodded understandingly. "And small-town museums seem to struggle so. People have no idea how fascinating local history can be. I remember thinking the sign meant that the museum was open twenty-four hours a day. On the other hand, the unique name makes Livermore Museum Now Open impossible to forget. It's a pleasure to meet you, Ms. Fineworth. I recognized you immediately from the society pages in *The Small Town Rag*."

Carlotta relaxed and smiled. "Why, how sweet you are, my dear! Yes, the paparazzi quite follow me everywhere. What else have you heard about me, my dear? Excuse me, but I so rarely get to mix with just ordinary people."

Leslie didn't mind the 'just ordinary people' remark. "They say that Livermore wouldn't be what it is today without you, Ms. Fineworth. It's such a wonderful city with its historic cattle markets and breathtaking cowboy atmosphere. One of my favorite things to do is to attend the 4-H auctions and watch the auctioneer sell the animals that the children raise for the local butcher shops. You were instrumental in arranging that some of that meat goes to feed the poor, were you not?"

"My, dear, how well-spoken you are for one so young. Your parents must be very proud of you. As to helping to feed the poor, I am particularly proud of that accomplishment. I had to overcome the butchers' unions to get it through, no small feat, I assure you. We compromised by donating only sausages and hamburger made from meat so high in fat, it isn't even sold to real people." Carlotta was getting to like this Leslie Tomatiny person. "Ms. Toma—may call you Leslie, my dear? Meaning no disrespect—"

"Not at all, Ms. Fineworth," Leslie answered. She was used to disrespect.

Carlotta went on. "My dear, I won't pretend that I didn't come into this store *specifically* to talk to you. Ordinarily, I shop at Secureway, where the prices are more reasonable than in these privately owned stores. I am here today, dear, because we at Livermore Museum Now Open, are very impressed with your produce displays. *The Local Gazette* provided the board with copies of the photos of *The Pyramids of Giza*, *Winged Victory*, and

Hoover Dam. What genius! What inspiration! Why, your displays could put Livermore on the map!"

That Carlotta Fineworth, curator of the LMNO, knew about Ye Olde Grocery's fruit displays was a real compliment to Leslie's talent. There were lots of artists in Livermore, mostly because there was almost nothing to do there—people had to reserve a seat to watch a Little League game.

"Why, I had no idea that LMNO knew about me," cried Leslie.

Ms. Fineworth continued to talk. "The reason I am here, dear girl, is to discuss exhibiting photographs of your produce displays at the Livermore Museum Now Open. We would be pleased if you could create a new display for the exhibit. I am sure we could find someone to donate whatever produce you might need. Some of the board members wanted you to do our historic Independence Hall.

One of her fruit displays in a museum! Leslie's excitement was exploding inside her quiet exterior.

Leslie smiled up at the old woman. "Ms. Fineworth, this is all so very thrilling. Please, let me show you my latest creation. It's a little risqué, I'll admit, but it sells a lot of zucchini, which can be hard to unload."

Leslie stepped aside and flourished the zucchini she still held toward *Zucchini on Parade*.

Carlotta hesitated and then walked around the zucchini display, frowning. After a single pass, Carlotta abruptly stopped, turned her back to the zucchini, and addressed Leslie.

"It is a bit unusual. Interesting, but—unusual. I suppose this is what they refer to as 'modern art,'" she said. She looked at the zucchini that Leslie held in her hand and leaned forward to whisper.

"My dear, all that zucchini pointing up—it might be construed as 'phallic.' Do you know what 'phallic' means, my dear?"

Leslie replied, "I am well aware of the meaning of the word 'phallic.' Renowned archeologists and historians have confirmed that phallic symbols have existed throughout time in every known culture in every part of the world. Ancient carvings and paintings depicted Egyptian pharaohs in a state of arou—" As she spoke, she punctuated her points with the zucchini.

Ms. Fineworth interrupted her. "Stop, my dear, stop! Put down that damned vegetable before you hurt yourself! You seem to have an un-natural interest in things that may be described as 'phallic.' Shame on you, young lady! Be ashamed! *The Local Gazette* has always been a radi-cal publication, churning out smut and articles that would shock bra-zen prostitutes who wear scanty garments in the coldest of weather, but, young lady, I assure you, the Livermore Museum Now Open does not display smut!"

Carlotta Fineworth wheeled her cart around and walked away. When she got to the door, she abandoned the cart and rushed out.

Boy, did I blow that, Leslie thought. *Still*, she thought. Still, it felt great that the curator of the museum had come in specifically to see her.

Leslie hoped to hear from Carlotta Fineworth. She waited six months and then gave up. Meanwhile, Leslie's mother allowed a drifter to move into the miserable, old house because he promised to get her free liquor once he landed a job as a bartender. When the drifter started drifting around Leslie, Leslie decided to do something she should have done the day she turned eighteen. She would move out. But Leslie couldn't possibly get her own place on what Ye Olde Grocery paid her.

Fortunately, things were heating up with Larger Billie. Larger Billie could loan her enough money to move. But would he do it? One morning, after she'd cried all night, she found the courage to ask. She rushed in to work and threw her arms around him.

"Oh, Larger—Larger, darling—my mother and her shockingly inap-propriate, sawdust-headed husband have taken in a border who sleeps on the couch. Because he does not pay utilities, they refuse to allow him to shower, although they do let him drink their water, which he slurps out of the faucet. Larger, I must get out. I am leaving Livermore—and Ye Olde Grocery."

Larger Billie was fast falling in love with the lonely young woman. It was the "darling" that did it. No woman had ever called him darling before. Larger Billie paid her as much as he could, but he barely made a profit. Most people shopped at the large-scale corporate controlled gro-cery stores that could offer better prices.

"Leslie, Leslie, you don't have to leave. The solution is obvious. I've been wanting to ask you this, for so long."

Billie struggled to get down on one knee. He took Leslie's small, white hand in his large, hairy one.

"Leslie…Leslie, my love—"

Leslie gasped. "Yes? Yes, Larger?"

"Leslie—will you move into my apartment?"

He would have been a wonderful roommate—he was clean, considerate, an adequate lover, and willing to load the dishwasher. But Leslie turned him down. Like Mr. Bottomly, her mother loved celebrity judge shows, and Leslie knew the dangers of roommates.

"No, Larger. I appreciate the offer, but I cannot risk having to sue you on national television because you kicked me out of your apartment."

Larger Billie looked confused.

Leslie went on, "Larger, I am leaving Livermore. I'm leaving Livermore because I hate this city even more than I care for you. By the way, I think that Ye Olde Grocery may suffer an economic hit when you lose the customers who shopped here just to see the new fruit displays. I'll need my back pay as soon as possible and, if you can lend me a hundred bucks, it would sure help."

Larger Billie wept as he counted a hundred dollars from the cash register.

Leslie left her mother a note:

Dear Mom,
Don't even look for me—Love, Leslie.

Her mother crumpled the note and threw it away.

With the extra money from Larger and her scant savings, Leslie rented a tiny illegal apartment that was really an underground bomb shelter built fifty years ago to protect against atomic fallout. Leslie's new home was in Oakland, but she wanted to shake off the old Leslie, and she refused to give Larger Billie her address. He tried to find her, but the bomb shelter was well hidden, and the owner kept its existence a careful secret because the city, county, and state would have fined his ass off for violating safety codes and nonpayment of property taxes.

Only a week after moving in, Leslie found a job doing research and shelving books at the Alameda County Library. Leslie was antisocial, bookish, and bright—the head librarian knew as soon as she saw her that she was perfect for working in a library.

Leslie loved her new job. She had her own desk and a nameplate that said Ms. Leslie Tomatiny. She loved her independence and the solid quiet of the bomb shelter. Things were really looking up.

On the way to work one morning, Leslie noticed a poster in the window of a pancake restaurant, advertising an adult-education class at Millard Fillmore Elementary-Adult Education in Oakland. Leslie admired the photo of Professor Jud Roy Lebowitz. Professor Lebowitz looked clean and well educated. He did not look like a man who grew up in a miserable old house like Leslie's mother's.

"And he's so much smaller than Larger Billie!" Leslie spoke without thinking. She wrote down the information about the class in the little green notebook she always carried.

Leslie had no real friends and was usually alone on holidays. Her favorite pastime was reliving her past mistakes.

Leslie wrote dull, deadly stuff that most people daydreamed through.

CHAPTER 10

Peppy Zipline

● ● ●

JOLLIE WHISTLED FROM HIS CLOUD at the beautiful redheaded woman reclining on a sheepskin rug. Her creamy skin glowed in the soft, dim light.

When Peppy read her romance novels, she wore white lace panties and sat by the fire with her leggy shadow and a stuffed bunny. She was thirty-two but looked younger.

"With my flowing red hair, lime-green eyes, and full, womanly breasts, I am the soul of the perfect female literary character," she was fond of saying. "Men cannot help but look. Although I am innocent of doing anything to attract attention, I am the victim of unwanted attention wherever I go. Women resent me—I have no female friends."

Peppy's parents worked at Home Repo in Oakland, where Peppy grew up. Her father worked in the plumbing department, and her mother worked in the pest-control section, which Mrs. Zipline called "The Aisle of Death."

"I work in the Aisle of Death," she would say, and then bray a laugh.

"She kills me," Mr. Zipline would say, and then laugh in turn. Neither of Peppy's parents had good teeth. They were best at giving people something to talk about.

Mr. and Mrs. Zipline were inordinately proud of their daughter because she was so beautiful. People automatically liked Peppy. They liked to pinch her cheeks or smooth her hair; they wanted to touch and pet her. Peppy was as irresistible as a soft, round kitten. Her parents called her The Baby until she was twelve years old.

"You're a pretty little thing—just look at this pretty little girl. She's going to be a real heartbreaker. Smile, honey, smile. Honey, lemmee see you smile."

"Go on, honey. Give the nice lady a smile. She's shy," Mrs. Zipline would say.

"Peppy, your mother told you to smile," her father would command. "Don't be rude."

Peppy didn't want to smile. She resented being told what to do with her body parts, but her parents cared more about being nice to other people than about their daughter's discomfort. As Peppy grew up, she got used to it. By the time she was grown up, she expected it.

On her eighteenth birthday, Peppy realized that she could finally get away from her jerk parents and their comedy routine about Home Repo's "Aisle of Death." The problem was that she had nowhere to go. The subway would be her magic carpet. While her parents were out buying her a grocery-store birthday cake, she snuck out.

"See you later," she whispered and then took the long walk to the subway station.

San Francisco was a mere half hour away, and Peppy's parents would think she was out shoplifting clothes that she couldn't afford but deserved anyway because she was good looking. Peppy never had any money. Her father thought she was too good to work. He liked to say that she'd never have to work because she was "destined to marry rich."

It was December, a cold December night. Downtown San Francisco wore costume jewelry lights, and Peppy's red hair snapped with electricity. She walked slowly by the shops, admiring the swell of her breasts in the store windows.

Years later, Peppy would tell her dates what happened the night of her eighteenth birthday. She always pretended to hesitate, then dabbed an imaginary tear before beginning.

"I met a man that night. He was a big man with a small part in a show that was playing at the Rhinoceros Theatre. The admission was free, so I went in to get out of the cold. It was a Christmas show, advertised as 'A

Gay Romp over the River and through the Wood.' It was supposed to be merry and all that, but it was so bad it stunk up the entire downtown area from Union Square to South of Market.

"The lead man, he was standing around in front of the theatre afterward. I recognized him right away, and he remembered me too. So, he asks how I liked the show and I say, 'Great!' Then I ask him if he was really a professional actor, and he tells me no. Turns out, he's a double agent disguised as an ambassador from England. He was so good, he didn't even have an accent. Anyway, he had to get back to his hotel room right away because 'A Gay Romp over the River and through the Wood was a just a setup for a case he was working on, and he had to make an emergency private phone call right away. He made me promise not to tell *anyone*. He wouldn't tell me his name because he said that most ambassadors are also double agents, so it wouldn't be a real name, anyway. So I went with him to his hotel because I'd never met a double agent or an actor or an ambassador before, and I was curious, plus he was kind of cute.

"He was so secret, he had to use his room key to ride the elevator, even. He said the entire floor was for secret investigations. As soon as we were in the room, he made the important phone call. 'Get me a pizza,' he said. It was obviously a secret code. I think the other agents were maybe torturing people in the other rooms. There's all this noise coming through the walls, and people are crying, 'Please, please.' People were knocking on doors and running down the hall. There's all this screaming and stuff, and some guy keeps shouting, 'I'm not a heretic!' Also, a dog was barking, and there was crashing and thumping, and electric drills and machinery sounds. All this time, the English ambassador-double-agent-actor guy acts like there's nothing happening. I started thinking maybe he'd brought me there because my mother used to shoplift rat poison from The Aisle of Death.

Then, I hear this woman yelling, 'Gotta Hawaiian! Did someone order a ham and pineapple?' The ambassador guy opens the door, and this woman rushes in and slams the door behind her really fast, like someone was chasing her. She was wearing a Hi-Ho Pizza and Away We Go T-shirt and a baseball hat.

'Special delivery,' she says and sets down a pizza. Then she takes off all her clothes. I swear to God, she really did that. 'Search me—I'm clean,' she says to the ambassador. 'Cash only—things are tight.' The ambassador-agent, he says, 'No problem—you always were a smart piece of pie. I like a woman who uses her head.' Then he searches her, real good too. No way was she hiding anything.

Then, the ambassador-actor guy, he gives her a message disguised as a coupon for two dollars off. They asked me to stay, but I got the hell out of there. I already knew too much. I'm pretty sure she was a secret agent, too. When I left, they were doing karate routines.

I couldn't take the elevator without the special key, so I had to go down the stairs. There's this whole bunch of policemen lined up on the stairs, waiting to go in. All the policemen ran past me, and then they run in. All I could hear was people screaming, and running, and things falling over. I hopped a BART train home, and my parents and I ate a Safeway cake they got for my birthday. It had dark-blue frosting that made our mouths all black. So there I was, eighteen years old and still at home. It took a lot of hard work, and some help from a Texas oil-well man, but two months later, I moved out for good."

At that point, Peppy would throw herself into her date's arms and make small kittenish sounds. Men never tired of comforting her. They didn't always hit a home run, but they usually got on base. The baseball games ended when the Texas oil-well man showed up.

The Texas oil-well man met Peppy at, of all places, Home Repo. She'd been wandering through the wood department, sniffing fresh pine and oak, when she saw him carefully inspecting a chainsaw that had been marked down 20 percent. At first, he seemed to struggle with the weight of the thing, and then he caught her eye and began swinging the chainsaw up and down, left and right, with seeming skill and ease. Impressed, Peppy lingered to watch.

"Howdy, little lady," the man said, winking. "Just checking this-a-hyaw saw…got a lot of big pines to clear—full a hundred acres of Texas land. I'm gon-na put in oil wells. Oil's the thing these days. Trees don' make money, no how."

"Well, money's good," said Peppy. "Trees are OK too, I guess. We never had any." What would have been the front and backyard of Peppy's parents' house was covered over with cement. Cement made better sense since it never needed water or mowing.

"Oh, Texas has a whole lotta trees. Yep, a whooooole lotta trees." The Texas oilman's eyes played up and down Peppy's lithe body. "How old y'all, baby girl?" he asked.

"I turned eighteen a week ago," she answered.

"That's just fine—just fine. You have an interest in wood?"

"No," said the beautiful girl. "I just like the way it smells. It smells fresh and clean."

"You still living at home with your mommy and daddy, baby girl?"

"Yeah. They both work here. I just came in to get some money from my mom," said Peppy. "She's busy. There's a gopher infestation through-out the Oakland Hills, and people are lining up at The Aisle of Death—I mean at the pest-control section."

"Waaaahl, hell. You don' want to bother yer momma when she's busy. Why don't I just give you a little cash? I'm in California on business for a while. Maybe we could be friends."

"You'd—you mean, you'd—give me money?" Peppy was amazed.

"Why, sure. I got lots a money. Say, how old are you, baby girl?" The Texan was reaching into his pocket for his wallet.

"I'm eighteen," Peppy told him again. Her eyes widened at the sight of the man's thick wallet.

The man counted five bills and handed them to Peppy. They totaled $500. Peppy bought all her clothes at Loss. Five hundred dollars was enough for four dresses, seven pairs of pants, ten shirts, a drawer full of lace panties and bras, and maybe a pair of shoes, or two pairs, even. The Texan gave Peppy a business card, and she put it into her purse.

After only two months, Peppy was living in her own apartment with her own furniture and a king-size bed, all courtesy of the Texas oil-well man. Unfortunately, the oil-well man turned out to be a cheapskate who only paid for food, clothes, travel, entertainment, utilities, garbage service, and rent. He was thirty-eight years old, but it seemed like a thousand to Peppy, and he harassed her for sex, sometimes twice a week. Peppy bore it for as long as she could and then gave him up and got a job at a fast-food place, and then a liquor store, and then a restaurant called Pancake Heaven. Because she was so beautiful, her customers tipped her well enough to pay her rent and other expenses that the Texan no longer covered. Her male customers were especially generous.

It seemed like Peppy's whole life was controlled by men. They never left her alone, and she never learned to be alone.

"I loved her," sniffed Jollie from the cloud. "Everyone else did too. She had…she had…*personality.*"

Jud Roy had just finished taping a flyer on to the window of the pancake restaurant when he turned around to see a beautiful red-haired woman watching him. Her breasts pressed against a tight-fitting waitress uniform. The front of the uniform read Pancake Heaven and had a picture of two fried eggs.

The young woman was staring at the poster. "Wow. Did that guy really write a book?"

Jud Roy cleared his throat. "I am the man of whom we speak." He bent over and kissed her syrupy hand.

"Allow me to introduce myself. I am Professor Jud Roy Lebowitz. I have written many things, so very many—why, it would be almost impossible to list them all."

Peppy had never met anyone like Jud Roy Lebowitz. He was obviously well educated; he even kissed her hand. He had actually written a book, and there was his picture right on the wall to prove it. He "introduced" himself—he was "Professor Jud Roy Lebowitz," an elegant gentleman, and not altogether bad-looking either.

"I'm Peppy Zipline. I'm a waitress here. Can anyone be in the class? I mean, um, I've never been to college."

Jud Roy leaned into her face and breathed in. She smelled like coffee and bacon. It was intoxicating.

"My class might be a bit challenging for you—but I charge very little for private tutoring sessions. Sometimes I charge nothing at all," he said in a sympathetic, bullshit voice.

"I usually write about my adventures. Last year, I traveled to Scandinavia with a guy named Fisk. He had red hair too. We would have had red-headed babies, but Fisk said we shouldn't because the world hated red-headed people, especially the babies," said Peppy.

Jud Roy held his chin in his hand. "Yes—yes, that is sadly enough true—but I do not hate red-headed people, even the ones with freckles. Travel writing interests me very much. It's a genre few have the courage to venture into."

"Well—I got talent, I really do. I really should take that class. I won the creative writing award at my high school. "

"Really? That is impressive—very."

A skinny teenager with pimples pushed an uncertain cart of dishes passed them. Peppy moved closer to Jud Roy.

"Did you see that man? Did you see the way he looked at me? It was like he couldn't help himself."

"He has what we refer to in the publishing business as a 'roving eye.'"

"He's been watching me a long time. I get scared sometimes. Men always watch me. Wherever I go."

"Yeah, well that can happen," said Jud Roy, unimpressed.

Peppy read the poster again. "If you wrote a book, I'm definitely gonna take that class. I'll do just what you say. I've never met a book-writer before, but I gotta a lot of talent, I really do."

"I'm sure you do. I felt there was something about you—something rare and wonderful." Jud Roy gave her a big, toothy smile. "Be on time—my classes are very popular, but I really want you. To win the creative writing award in high school, you must have great talent. I am always glad to tutor my very talented students."

"I got no money," Peppy said.

"Tut, tut! You do not have to pay me," said Jud Roy. "I do this sort of thing all the time, without recompense."

"Does the class get out after it gets dark? I might need someone to walk me back to the parking lot after class. It is my curse that wherever I go I am sexually harassed and even threatened with violence by wealthy men in powerful positions," she tearfully confided.

"I would be happy to escort you to your car," said Jud Roy.

Peppy wrote about sex. Her favorite pastime was lying in bed being afraid.

CHAPTER 11

Dino Quiet Room

● ● ●

Now and then Jollie tried to shape a bed from parts of his cloud, lay down, and pretend to watch the video like he used to watch TV. It took five minutes for the cloud bed to close over him. He poked his head out to watch Dino down below.

Dino Quiet Room's real name was Mary Lou Smith. She grew up in an average family with an average mother, father, and brother in a tract house that looked exactly like every other tract house in the neighborhood. Her brother tried not to be seen with her because her weight embarrassed him. Her mother, a former Miss Strawberry Queen, ignored her because she was unattractive. Her father, a well-dressed businessman, both ignored and despised her because she was overweight and unattractive and looked out of place at social functions with rich people. For years, Dino watched, waited, and hoped for someone to notice her, but people almost never did. Unattractive women are mostly invisible.

At twenty-five, Dino resembled a huge, overripe pineapple. She claimed to be a "goddess," and she draped herself in filmy, multi-patterned silk robes and walked with a mahogany staff topped with exotic feathers. In public, she ate raw broccoli and fish, but in private she ate whatever she wanted, which she justified by claiming that she needed extra energy to survive visits to the afterlife.

For a weirdo, Dino made a decent living. She told people not only who they had been reincarnated from but also who the person they were reincarnated from was reincarnated from and who that person was reincarnated from, and so on until the beginning of time, but to go back that far would cost more than anyone on earth could pay. Practically all her clients had spent at least one of their past lives as a Buddhist monk. Before making an appointment with clients, she always had them sign a release of liability form.

Release of Liability

I _____can prove I am not a robot. Furthermore, on this day and/or night of _____, (to include past and future time periods), in consideration of my participation at _____, I hereby release Dino Quiet Room from liability for loss, injuries, dismemberment, death, or damage to personal property that which may, or that which may not occur as a result of participation in the event of which we are speaking. Goddess Dino Quiet Room retains legal ownership of any and all secrets, to include those deemed illegal or horribly embarrassing. Your séance may be posted on social media.
Namaste.
(sign and date) _____
*For your personal safety and the safety of others, please leave all prescription medications at the door.

"Although I have yet to lose a client, some people are afraid to meet themselves in the form of, say, a camel or a lunatic in a cage, but it is the experience of a lifetime," she would tell people convincingly and present the liability form.

Lost people looking for new identities swore by her powers. She seemed sincere. Dino always ended the sessions with a warm hug, open and free. She was not afraid to press her breasts against her clients, in fact she encouraged them to bury their faces into the deep cleavage between her breasts and cry. Dino also revealed her magical self to people who were not clients. Before each meal, she would fold her hands on the table and sit in perfect silence, breathing heavily, and waving her hands over her food. After a few moments, she would mumble incoherent things, quietly at first, and then her voice grew louder, and louder still with scattered emotion, until the sounds she made ranged from the squeak of a guinea pig to that of a pig. It lasted about three minutes, and people were always impressed. Restaurants barred her after a single performance, but no one ever forgot she had been there.

Dino had a small stable of regular clients, but now and then, she needed to replenish her stock, so she would search local papers for singles' parties, art exhibits, and any event with lots of people. Wedding receptions were her favorite. An especially memorable one was Avi Weiner and Sarah Adelman's reception at Le Grand Hotel on Pine Street—Dino didn't pick up any paying clients there, but she did meet a man named Jud Roy Lebowitz.

"The wedding," Jollie mumbled to himself. "Maybe Peppy will die one day and join me on my cloud. That would be heaven."

Dino always tried to arrive at wedding receptions during the father-daughter dance, when all of the guests were bored. Timing was essential if her visit was going to take the maximum effect. In the middle of Sarah and her father's stumbly waltz, she hefted herself onto a table in the front of the dance floor and waved her feathered staff about. It looked like she was conducting the disc jockey, but the timing was all wrong. After she had everyone's attention, she asked for quiet and a microphone.

"Where are you now, soul-searchers, seekers of distant stars, of monologues distinct, and not easily tolerated? Is there such a thing as a holiday? If we go back, then forward, to the beginning, and the end, if we circle left, then right, until we cover all directions of all time, will we find anything worth discussing? I appear to you now in the form of Dino Quiet Room, a rare goddess who specializes in conjuring the living dead that do not fall into the category of zombie. Yes, you heard me right—the living dead, again, not to be confused with zombies, but those who have died and then awakened in another body as opposed to the wretched, decrepit one they died in."

There was a hushed groan of disappointment that there would be no zombies. Hiring actors to play zombies at weddings and receptions was becoming more and more popular because it livened things up. Someone hired one for a funeral once, but it had upset people and the funeral homes banned it.

"I speak not of zombies but of reincarnation. 'What is reincarnation?' you ask. I'm glad you did. Never be afraid ask. Remember, there are those who sleep even through the unholy sound of leaf blowers. The *Oxford Dictionary* defines reincarnation as 'the rebirth of a soul in a new body.' Who among you does not want a new body? No one I see here. Nevertheless, in good conscience, I must advise you that reincarnation is not the quick fix to being ugly or dead as it would seem to be. I know a soul who, after a stout, vigorous life of ninety-six years, woke up to find himself in a beetle body that survived a week and then became a trout who went from a fish farm in Oregon to a fish tank in a restaurant in Manhattan. Within six months, that poor man had been reincarnated thirty seven times into twenty-five different species. I used to visit him but stopped after his last life because he complained so much. I hope I have made myself clear. Clarity is to the mind as the soul is to beauty."

Dino stared down at the dance floor and gave a long, slow sigh before continuing.

"Yes, he complained too much and lost all of his friends. Perhaps he feared death, but death takes no effort at all. I have died many times, and it is easily accomplished. It comes when we least expect it, it brings rest, and it eases pain. Death is as common as birth and should be celebrated, not feared. The young bride will die, the young groom will die, and their parents, family, and all of the guests will die. Even the little flower girl will one day die, probably as a dusty, wrinkled hag instead of the fresh-faced five-year-old we delight in today. Would we delight in the hag? Would we stroke the old, gray head, kiss the wrinkled cheek, or dress her crooked body in pretty clothes? Where will she be when her time comes? The lucky will die peacefully, surrounded by loved ones. The unlucky will die alone, in mental or physical pain. The majority will die in some ordinary way hardly worth mentioning—but the good news is that, while we may be unhappy about dying at the time, we can find comfort in the certainty of reincarnation. Reincarnation means eternal life, and eternal chances of being that one in a million, of having wealth, fame, of being thin or having good hair. Perhaps the sorry life one clings to may change into a life of joy and prosperity. You doubt me—you ask, 'what can she know?' Though it be bliss in a pork chop tree, I know the certainty of an afterlife."

Dino lifted her arms into a high arch. The wedding photographers captured the pose beautifully. After the photograph, Dino wound up her speech by saying, "For those hungry for enlightenment, which makes everything better, my price list is on the back of my cards. Cash only. Please line up for a free sample."

She climbed down from the table and waited.

Dino always offered a demonstration of her powers. At Avi and Sarah's wedding reception, she revealed a potato chip to be Sarah's dead hamster, Patsy, come back as a potato that was turned into a chip. She identified an entire family as a former marching band that played over two million years ago, using sticks and rocks. She predicted that, before the year was over, Avi's grandmother would die and be reincarnated into a wealthy heir's baby. Some of the guests lined up to congratulate the old woman, who soon be rich. Afterward, Dino walked about the room, introducing herself and passing out business cards that read as follows:

Substantial Medium Dino Quiet Room, Conjures the Dead
Call Dino Quiet Room at (925) 831-1212
1223 Eighteenth Street, Apt. 64, Oakland, CA
Cash Only
Clients required to sign Release of Liability
This Establishment Does Not Conjure Zombies

It was at Avi and Sarah's reception that Dino met Jud Roy Lebowitz. Jud Roy didn't know Avi and Sarah, but he had been invited to the wedding on account of his father, Dr. Harvey Lebowitz, whom Sarah's great-uncle Dr. Henky Lebowitz claimed was a distant cousin.

Dino approached Jud Roy.

"My card—in celebration of the wedding. There's a coupon on the back—meet a former life for only fifty bucks."

He needed one more student to make ten people for the class, and he warmly grasped her surprised hand.

"So very, very happy to meet you, Dino. Dino Quiet Room is it? Oh, yes, it's here on your card. My, you should put a photo of yourself on your card. I've never seen such pretty eyes!"

"People always notice eyes. They are the windows of the soul. Even the blind show themselves through their eyes."

Jud Roy said, "Windows—and eyes—a remarkable simile—I mean, metaphor—or, um—say, are you a writer by trade?"

"Because I do not know your name, I will call you Tall, Dark, and Handsome Stranger at a Wedding. Tall, Dark and Handsome Stranger at a Wedding, I have many trades. I have many gifts," Dino murmured.

Jud Roy flashed her a charming smile. "I can always tell a gifted writer. But I do not want to be a stranger to *you*, dear lady. Allow me to introduce myself. I am Professor Jud Roy Lebowitz, and I am a writer by trade. I teach creative writing at Millard Fillmore Elementary-Adult Education, right here in Oakland. Let me give you a flyer. I have a feeling about you."

"Jud Roy Lebowitz, I am happy to make your present life's acquaintance."

"Dino, I would truly love to have you in my class. As I said, I have a feeling about you."

"Jud Roy Lebowitz, it is probable that I should record my thoughts and not write them down on paper, where they can be easily found. It could be dangerous. First, I shall consult the spirits regarding the class. They will advise me as to what to do. Meanwhile, perhaps you or your significant other would like a free opportunity to speak to a dead person?"

"I don't know any dead people I want to talk to. And I have others but none of them significant."

"Jud Roy Lebowitz, nonsignificant others are also welcome. And you might enjoy talking to dead strangers. Do you have fifty bucks, cash?"

"Maybe—"

"Then I will take your flyer."

Jud Roy gave her a flyer. Like most people, he thought that Dino was a self-absorbed lump of bullshit. He never called for a consultation, but Golam, Sarah's father, did. Dino stubbed her toe painfully when she hurried out of the shower to answer her phone.

"Ms. Quiet Room?"

"Yes?" Dino snapped. She was jumping around naked on one foot.

"This is Golam Adelman, Sarah's father, from the wedding reception."

Dino stopped jumping and lowered her voice. "Yes, this is Goddess Quiet Room. I am not surprised to hear from you, Golam Alderman. When I bore witness to your dance with your daughter, I felt your inner struggle and pain."

"The things you claimed at the wedding…you say you can see into the past? That you can name previous lives?"

"Yes, Golam Adelman, I can. Are you interested in a consultation?"

"I may be. You say that your profession provides you a living? That people pay money for your readings?"

"Yes, Golam Adelman. You will meet yourself several times over and, in the end, know your own soul from the beginning to the present time. Of course, the further back you go, the more effort, and therefore the more money, it takes."

"I have one of your coupons here that says you do readings for fifty dollars cash."

"A fifty-dollar reading goes back only one life," Dino warned. "But I can feel that your need extends beyond fifty doll—er, beyond the ordinary. I feel that your past is a long one, long and arduous, with many lives and much travel. Tell me, Golam Adelman, have you ever wanted to be a woman?"

"What? No! Let's get back to the séance. Do you always insist on cash, Ms. Quiet Room? I only ask because I get a lot of bonus points on my American Express," Mr. Adelman explained.

"I never touch plastic, Golam Adelman," said Dino. "It is an evil thing."

"Ah, I see…but of course it is. I would like to schedule an appointment with you—perhaps several. I am a wealthy man, Ms. Quiet Room, and I can pay cash, with or without a coupon. By the way, is Dino Quiet Room your real name?"

"It is my goddess name," explained Dino. "It is more than real, for it extends throughout time."

"Throughout time? How long have you been conducting séances for cash money, Ms. Quiet Room?"

"Many, many years. More than I know."

"Do you file your taxes under Dino Quiet Room or some other name?"

"Um..."

"Speak up, Ms. Quiet Room. This is Dino Quiet Room isn't it? The woman who was at my daughter's wedding today, Saturday, the fourth of March, two thousand and fifteen?"

Dino heard rapid clicking sounds. She hung up and spent the evening watching out the window. She never saw Mr. Adelman again, or heard from anyone who claimed to have seen her at Avi and Sarah's wedding.

Dino's favorite pastime was fantasizing about sleeping with Gandhi, except that she pictured him with hair and wearing a red tie and a gray pinstriped suit.

She wrote strange, mystical stuff that nobody understood.

CHAPTER 12

Jollie Inch

● ● ●

THE READER HAS ALREADY MET Jollie, but further description may provide insight and create compassion for our protagonist.

Jollie was a narcissist to the infinite power. To tenderhearted bliss-ninnies, Jollie's arrogance disguised an abusive childhood, a sexual-identity crisis, or perhaps, premature toilet training. It did not. He was a hot air balloon that spit down on everything it passed over, and most people wanted to beat the hell out of him—but he did have some good qualities. For example, he was not shy. Also, no matter how much a person tried, he was not easy to forget.

Jollie wrote about himself. When he wasn't writing, his favorite pastime was thinking about how people would admire what he would write.

CHAPTER 13

The Students Read

● ● ●

Jud Roy Lebowitz wore a brand new green-checked sports coat and pressed Levis. "Good evening. I am Professor Jud Roy Lebowitz. This is Creative Writing. We meet Mondays, Wednesdays, and Fridays from five to seven. I begin.

"The first thing to remember is that to write creatively, you must forget everything you have ever learned. Write whatever you want—own your imagination. I will not interfere with binding words—and in spite of what you've heard, there *is* such a thing as a dumb question, so think well before you ask. Next class, bring something to read—anything at all. For now, I want you to write down what writing experience you have, why you are here, a brief biography, your likes and dislikes, and what you expect from the class. Be detailed. You have until seven o'clock to finish."

Professor Lebowitz sat down and stared at the clock, willing it to move faster.

Wednesday was the first evening the students read aloud. Most of the students secretly wanted to write about their painful, pitiful histories and read them aloud to the rest of the class. They all imagined that their readings would evoke tears and consolation.

With the exception of Leslie, Dino, Peppy, and Jollie, everyone wrote odes.

One woman wrote an ode about the truth.

Ode to the Truth about Truth

We're all going to die, and there's nothing we can do about it.
Alone, we go,
Leaving our idiot children
to die too.
That is all we know and all we need to know.

Another woman wrote an ode about her wretched studio apartment.

Ode to My Wretched Studio Apartment

Small made smaller by the dirt that darkens the windowsill.
Outside, the crazy man sings words most foul.
My master does not, will not permit my escape.
Rent control is my bondage
And my salvation.

A man wrote, "Ode to Flowing Red Hair, Lime-Green Eyes, and Full, Womanly Breasts," about the elusive Peppy.

Ode to Flowing Red Hair, Lime-Green Eyes,
and Full, Womanly Breasts

Peppy, Peppy, please accept me.
I have more money than God.
I have more wisdom than Confucius.
I have more real estate than the United States government.
I am a liar.

Jollie snorted. There were weak smiles from three women trained to lie for politeness's sake. The rest of the class looked down at their shoes.

In the middle of one shy lady's ode about her divorce attorney, Jollie stood up and announced, "I will refrain from presenting my essay until everyone else has finished."

Throughout the readings, Jud Roy had been making the necessary teacher comments like, "Hm…Ah…Yes." Finally, there were only four students left to read. Jud Roy hid a yawn.

"Leslie? What do you have for us?"

Leslie had written a journalistic article entitled "Ye Olde Grocery Store, We Hardly Knew Ye."

Ye Olde Grocery Store, We Hardly Knew Ye

Ye Olde Grocery Store, a fixture on Main Street in Livermore since 1958, shut its doors today after being indicted for failure to pay payroll taxes, sales and use taxes, environmental taxes, transportation taxes, insurance taxes, and other taxes and fees not yet disclosed. The owner, William Penny, also known as Larger Billie, claimed he was really, really sorry, but he just couldn't figure out the paperwork. He was sentenced to fines totaling the value of the grocery store and five years' community service cleaning law offices who qualify as charity organizations.

Jud Roy scratched his chin. "Hm. Excellent, Leslie, excellent. The poems were getting very tiresome. If I'd had to hear another one, I would've thrown up." The professor shot a withering glance at the man who had written "Tweet a Little Birdie."

"That was the best one so far," a banana-color-haired woman whispered to Leslie. "It was much better than my ode to the fucked-up calendar app on my iPhone. I thought the rape of the innocent grocery store by a heartless, indifferent government very stimulating. To present the theme as a newspaper article was brave."

The banana-color-haired woman waited for a reply, but Leslie was giving all of her attention to Dino Quiet Room, who had just stood up to read.

"Jud Roy Lebowitz, my piece will have more effect if everyone closes their eyes and leans their heads back. May we can turn off the light?"

She looked at Jud Roy, who nodded. Dino fixed her eyes on the person sitting nearest the light switch until he got up and flipped it off. About half the class closed their eyes. Some of the students went to sleep.

Metaphysical Essay of Federico Fellini and Jesus Christ

Fellini—was he once Christ? Was Christ once Fellini? Those who have met them both are convinced it is true. I knew them, and I can tell you that they were both bearded. And they spoke of the same God.

That was all. Nobody knew what the hell she was talking about. The man turned on the light and everyone looked at one another. Jollie rolled his eyes.

"What the hell was that?" he opined and embarrassed the class by voicing what they'd all been thinking.

Jud Roy cleared his throat. "Thank you—what was your name again?"

"Jud Roy Lebowitz, I call my life form Dino Quiet Room," she answered. "We met at Avi and Sarah's wedding reception."

"Ah! But of course I remember you and our evening together, Dino. I want to acknowledge that it took a lot of courage to write that. I know it will give us pause for thought." He paused to think. "Um, excellent work. Who's next?"

When the beautiful Peppy stood up, everyone stared. Peppy read the first chapter from her embarrassingly pornographic novel about her trip to Denmark:

My Embarrassingly Pornographic Novel
about My Trip to Denmark

How still the night, the night! I hear a tap on my window, a male voice mumbles in Dutch. The voice grows louder!

Scandinavia is such a strange country, rife with natural blondes and Swedes. Because of my flowing red hair, lime-green eyes, and full, womanly breasts, the tall, striking Vikings wanted me desperately. Men are evil bastards.

The evil bastards got eviler as the story went on. By the third page, everyone was thoroughly embarrassed. When Peppy finished, after a moment of silence, the class clapped enthusiastically and admired Peppy's breasts, which were, in fact, quite large. The piece had fulfilled its promise and could only be regarded as a great success.

"Thank you, Peppy," said Jud Roy. "Thank you very much. That was wonderful." He smiled a genuine smile.

"I have one comment," Leslie said. "Although it does have blondes and Swedes, Scandinavia isn't a country." Most of the class gave her a dirty look.

"Women—they know as much about geography as they do about football," a burly man with a crooked nose said out loud.

The class laughed. Leslie pushed the rude comment into the crowded part of her mind reserved for painful memories.

Peppy knew she'd made a big hit. When she sat back down, Jud Roy caught her eye and winked at her. Everyone saw. They'd been waiting for his reaction.

Jollie leaned out of his cloud. "I never get tired of this," he said.

Down below, Jollie stood up to read. Instead of reading from his seat, he walked slowly to the front of the class. He wore his power-red Hermes tie.

Jollie gave a long "Hhhhhem!"

"My work, about myself, which I am sure you will all enjoy, is indeed about myself. I always write about myself—the subject never fails to enlighten. I will now read from my essay entitled 'About Myself. My Own Naked Reflection.'"

About Myself: My Own Naked Reflection

First...the Awakening. I always awaken at eleven a.m. I awaken every morning at that exact same time, even though I do not use an alarm clock—imagine! I awaken in the nude. I am unafraid to show my body. If the law permitted, I would show it to you now— the sight is a pleasing one. Head and shoulders, chest, flat stomach, strong arms and legs—pleasing, without art or artifact. Now, feast your mind's eye as I read further. As I read about myself—my own naked reflection, as observed by myself looking in a full-length mirror at myself. I begin with the ten perfect toes.

As the title indicated, Jollie's fifteen-page essay was a description of his own naked body. He embellished his reading with hand gestures, operatic rises and falls, and awkward voice inflections and finished with a dignified crescendo-like shout. At the close of his essay, he made four bows, one to the right side of the class, one to the left, one to the middle, and the last to Jud Roy Lebowitz.

The room was still. For a full five minutes, nobody moved.

Jud Roy Lebowitz finally spoke, because somebody had to say something, and he was the teacher, damn the luck.

"Jollie, your work stands alone. That description of your scrotum left me...why, I could actually see it! An excellent use of 'show don't tell.'"

"I myself thought it was well drawn," said Jollie proudly. "What did you think about the part about the rise and fall of my biceps? Speaking for myself, I enjoyed that piece most."

The lady who had written a limerick entitled "I Loved You Once and Never Again" raised her hand.

"Personally, I thought the description, 'masculine mountains of muscle made memorable' was remarkable."

Peppy shocked everyone by adding, "Parts of the essay could have been longer. I was disappointed when it was over."

"Then I will lengthen it," said Jollie. "So as not to disappoint you." His heart skipped a beat. Everyone stared down at the floor.

Jud Roy ended the class, which, thanks to Jollie's paper, got out at seven forty-five instead of seven.

"Remarkable work, students. I can't wait for next week."

"Nor I," Jollie said aloud, smiling. Jollie winked at the professor.

"Don't we have any homework?" asked Leslie flatly. "The flyer indicated this was a challenging class."

Jud Roy passed out copies of an exercise in diagramming sentences that he had found on the regular teacher's desk.

"I have some sentence diagrams here—see if you can pick out the nouns, verbs, adjectives, and what used to be known as 'adverbs'—some of the older students may remember what adverbs are. Adverbs are words that end in *l-y*. Words like jolly, jingly, holy, or holly—most Christmas words are adverbs."

Only Leslie took a paper. All the students except one shuffled out. As Jud Roy had feared, Jollie stayed after class.

"I thought I should tell you about my writing experience. Did I mention that I wrote my autobiography when I was only five years old? Indeed. I have quite a lot of experience as a writer. When I was eight, my school recognized me as a prodigy. Oh, yes. My teacher, Ms. Big Sky, a sensitive, artistic woman, called my father and told him to come right away. Ordinarily, I take classes at only name-brand universities, but I have some big business deals in the area just now, so I had to settle for Millard Fillmore. I'd like to hear more of your thoughts on 'About Myself—My Own Naked Reflection.' I've had so much interest from various publishers, I'm thinking about expanding it into a novel. A kind of *tour de farce*."

Jud Roy tried to look busy. "Atta boy. Sounds wonderful. Use lots of adverbs."

"I plan to," Jollie assured him. "Perhaps I will submit additional work to you. As I said, I'd like hear your thoughts."

The professor yawned. He neither noticed nor cared that Jollie left without saying good-bye. As soon as he was gone, Jud Roy rushed off to look for Peppy, who by that time, was waggling through the parking lot.

CHAPTER 14

The Three Musketeers

• • •

THE CLASS ENDED AT SEVEN, when the freeways choked on commuter traffic and frustrated drivers wept. Leslie came up with the idea of forming writing groups and meeting after class in the school's empty classrooms until the freeways cleared. Just like in high school, the braver, more popular students quickly formed groups and the leftover scraps made do with each another. After a half hour, everyone was part of a group except for Leslie, Dino, Peppy, and Jollie.

Leslie approached Dino because she liked her pineapple shape. Leslie had come up with a joke that she was sure would be a hit.

"Hi. I'm Leslie Tomatiny. Your observations about the similarities between Jesus Christ and Fellini were, uh, interesting. You could add that because Fellini was reincarnated from Jesus Christ, Fellini might have named his first movie *Forgive Us Our Sinemas*. Get it? Like…sins…cinemas? Like Fellini made a movie so bad it was a sin? See what I mean? Pretty funny, huh?"

Dino stared at Leslie, silently considering her advice. Leslie shifted her eyes away and stumbled into a table that wasn't there.

The round woman spoke in a dull monotone. "Leslie Tomatiny, I thank you for your counsel, but I must decline your very interesting suggestion because neither Jesus Christ nor Gandhi ever laughed. I knew a mystic once that you remind me of, a mystic whose spirit I am sure dwells in you, crouched in the darkness of your nether regions. You feel this man, and he feels you. Let me give you a card. Fifty dollars, cash, for new clients." Dino handed Leslie her card, which Leslie carefully read.

"Thank you, but reincarnation is only a theory with no basis in fact. History shows that almost all theories are ridiculous, sloppy-minded non-sense that some nincompoop concocted to get attention," Leslie said honestly.

Dino wasn't offended. She knew that an insecure mess like Leslie would come around. Her type always did.

Jollie and Peppy each stood alone on either side of the room. Their eyes met briefly. Jollie raised an eyebrow, and Peppy skittered over to Leslie and Dino.

"Come on," she hissed, "let's form a group and get out of here before that naked-reflection guy goes for me. Anybody want a drink? It's ladies night at the Hoegaarden."

"It's always ladies night at the Hoegaarden," Leslie said. "But a drink sounds good to me."

Dino glanced briefly at Jollie, who gave her a crooked smile. "Peppy Zipline and Leslie Tomatiny, spirits are the answer to our prayers," she agreed.

The three women rushed to the parking lot. Jollie stroked his Hermes tie. He followed coolly behind them. *No desperate fool I*, he thought. The women piled into Peppy's car and drove to the bar, only three blocks away.

"Hey, ladies!" Jollie called to them from his cloud. He hadn't liked them much when he was alive, but that was then, and this was now.

The Hoegaarden fairly burst with customers, most of whom were men. Three months ago, the owner had put up a sign that read Free Beer to Topless Ladies. It was supposed to be a joke, but several women pro-tested the sign by going to the bar, removing their shirts and bras, and demanding free beer. Business was great, so much so that the owner kept the sign up indefinitely.

Peppy, Leslie, and Dino squeezed into a tight table near the bathroom door. A bored, elderly disc jockey played loud music that was heavy on the base and light on the vocals.

Peppy eyed the topless ladies nuzzling their foamy beers. "I'd have at least held out for a mixed cocktail," Peppy yelled over the music. "I mean, I don't think anyone would call me a prude or anything—"

"I'd like to see them try!" shouted Leslie. She hated being around really good-looking people.

"I suppose you'd show your tits to the world for a free beer!" Peppy shouted back.

"What?" hollered Dino.

The music changed and the bar went quiet.

"I said, I'll bet you'd show your tits to anyone for a free beer!" Peppy yelled again. Dino looked offended.

"Peppy Zipline, I do not reveal my nether regions for free spirits."

Everyone in the bar turned to look.

"I suggest you lower your voice," Leslie said to Peppy.

The music started up again.

A waiter approached their table and set a coconut filled with chilled pineapple juice, rum, white froth, and speared fruit on the table in front of Peppy.

"From the man at the end of the bar," he said.

The man at the end of the bar nodded to Peppy, who crossed her legs and sipped the drink.

"So, there's your mixed drink—enjoy," said Leslie.

She stared longingly at the tropical concoction and sighed. It was not the drink she wanted, but the experience of having it paid for by a stranger.

Five minutes passed, and the waiter returned and set a bowl-shaped glass of something pink, from which fog from dry ice spilled.

"From the man at the table to the far right," he said.

The man at the table to the far right raised his glass to Peppy. She leaned forward and cooled her face in the chilly fog before tasting the drink.

Dino rubbed her temples and fiercely meditated. Like Leslie, she suffered from the men's disinterest.

Leslie stared at Peppy and thought, *She is a distant star-diamond, and I am a cubic zirconia worth less than a dollar. I would probably do anyone for a free beer. Or for the experience itself.* She thought briefly of Larger Billie.

The waiter was there again.

"From the man standing near the pool table," he said, and set down a beer.

The man near the pool table saluted Peppy. It was Jollie.

"It might be best to leave—there's an all-night doughnut shop just around the corner," said Leslie. Peppy, Leslie, and Dino hurried out, turned a corner, and ducked into The Sweet Circle, a deserted doughnut shop. The air was warm and yeasty.

Jollie tried to follow them, but he could not reach the exit before the ladies disappeared around the corner. He took the ladies' corner table and drank the three drinks that Peppy had left. He waited awhile, hoping the women would return, and then went home.

The three women sat down and relaxed in the sugar-smelling quiet. Jelly doughnuts, glazed doughnuts, pink doughnuts, crullers, fritters, even croissants winkled at them from the glass counters. Everyone's a kid in a doughnut shop. The ladies sighed, feeling younger. What with the alcohol, the comforting warmth of the doughnuts, and the exercise they'd gotten from running away from Jollie, they would sleep like babies that night—but now, there was work to be done.

First, they discussed a name for their group.

"Leslie Tomatiny and Peppy Zipline, I have a perfect name—The Three-Sided Pyramid," stated Dino. "Our group will remind others of the pyramid's power and spirituality."

"Actually, pyramids have five si—" said Leslie.

"What about The Three Little Kittens?" Peppy interrupted.

"No way," objected Dino. She folded her arms over her protruding stomach.

Leslie decided it. "Let's go with The Three Musketeers. At least it's a book."

"Movie," corrected Peppy.

They all agreed to name the group The Three Musketeers.

With the exception of the Three Musketeers, everyone in the class wrote poetry. Poetry bored Jollie, and when it became apparent that the rest of the class would write nothing else, he crashed the Three

Musketeers' meetings. They didn't want him, but no matter where they went, he'd show up.

"Hey, I'm here. Next time, tell me what room we're going to be in, that way you won't have to wait to start. Did Dino take her nether regions home after class? No? Let's just start. She has no idea what's going on anyways. I made some copies of the essay I read in class today, 'Pepperoni Mama— What a Mother.' We'll want to spend a lot of time going over it. Make lots of notes on what you find the most interesting. Afterward, we'll discuss it, and then I'll talk about my history and how it relates to 'Pepperoni Mama.'"

The ladies' good manners prevented any of the three women from telling Jollie to go to hell. After five meetings they gave up trying to dodge him but kept the name The Three Musketeers, hoping that he would take a hint and leave. Instead, he made numerous attempts to change the name.

"How about One Man, Three Easy Pieces?" he suggested once, eyeing the three women. "One easy piece especially." Jollie smiled at Peppy. He stared boldly, hoping she would appreciate the compliment. Peppy blushed and giggled like a little girl, which emboldened Jollie to lean forward.

"My dear…when you are near…the angels cheer," he murmured. Jollie sat up nights composing daring comments.

"I don't get it," said Peppy. She snuck a little sniff at her underarm and giggled again.

Leslie had never blushed nor giggled in her life. Jollie's weirdness bothered her, and the fluid way the Musketeers came and went struck her as dangerous.

She suggested a fixed schedule. "Musketeers, we are becoming lax in our meetings. If we are to improve our writing skills, we must have discipline. Our meetings should start and end at predetermined times. I propose we meet immediately after class and stay exactly one and a half hours, until eight thirty, and then walk to the parking lot together."

She reminded everyone that they had to leave by nine, when the janitor locked everything up. Leslie always knew the details.

Peppy was very concerned about having to be out by nine o'clock.

"Does the nine o'clock curfew apply to the teachers too?" she asked.

Leslie corrected her. "Actually, *curfew* means that after a given time, one must stay inside, not leave to go outside. Curfew is usually implemented in times of danger, but it has also been used to curtail people's rights. For example, in 1939, Germany enacted a law that Jews had to stay inside after eight at night."

Peppy was shocked. "Jud Roy is Jewish. Are Jewish people allowed to go out after eight if they're in the United States?"

"Uh, yes. Unless they're children and their parents make them come home," Leslie said.

Dino looked thoughtful. "That is very interesting news, Leslie—that non-Jewish children are permitted by their parents to be out after eight in the evening."

"But Jud Roy is *a man*. He can stay out as long as he wants. I'm so glad," Peppy sighed.

Jollie sneered. "Who cares if the great professor gets to stay out after eight o'clock? You ask me, a person as ugly as him should stay inside twenty-four hours a day. You deserve someone a hell of a lot better than Jud Roy *Lebowitz*. Now, me, I was an athlete, you know. Oh, yes—football, baseball, soccer, boxing, tennis—my body is a lean, mean, fighting machine and countless people and women have told me so. You remember my essay, 'My Own Naked Reflection,' don't you?—of course you do. It is factual, I assure you, every word. But Jud Roy Lebowitz? Ha! You and him together would be like a marriage between a giraffe and an elephant. Where as I..." His eyes gazed into the triangle that separated Peppy's cleavage. How soft she was!

"Don't you mean 'you and he?'" asked Leslie, interrupting his thoughts.

"No, I mean him and Peppy, fool!" Jollie did not like to be corrected.

"But Jud Roy can stay out as long as he wants to," Peppy said again.

"Is it eight thirty yet?" asked Dino. "I have a séance at nine o'clock. A very interesting case. Ordinarily, I do not discuss my clients, but this woman is so very remarkable, I tell everyone. After our last session, I revealed that the poor lady had been reincarnated from not one but two people, Scandinavian Siamese twins, who were joined at the hip. The woman, of course, had a multiple-personality disorder. I am tracing the past lives of the Siamese twins tonight."

Leslie stated that reincarnation had no basis in fact. Peppy allowed that it might be, but only in cases of true love. Dino said that true love had no basis in fact, that it was pure instinct, and the dirty business of the nether regions. Jollie put his hand on Peppy's knee, which offended Leslie, who correctly remarked that Jollie was at least two inches shorter than Jud Roy. By eight thirty, they had accomplished nothing by way of writing, but traffic had cleared.

"Even then, I was impressed that Leslie noticed the difference in Jud Roy and my heights. She was such a stickler for detail," said Jollie. The cloud was getting soggy. He knew it would rain soon.

CHAPTER 15

Jealousy

● ● ●

JUD ROY LEBOWITZ COULD NOT stop thinking about Peppy and her essay, "My Embarrassingly Pornographic Novel about My Trip to Denmark." Until the students formed the writing groups, as promised, he had walked her to her car to protect her from men who might be lurking in the school parking lot. Now that the students were staying late, Peppy walked to the parking lot with Jollie, Leslie, and Dino. The idea of Jollie spending time with three women, one of them a gorgeous redhead drove Jud Roy crazy. During one of the Musketeers' walks to the parking lot, Peppy confided that she was looking for a new job.

"I've been at Pancake Heaven for almost three months now, but men just won't leave me alone," she confessed. "For example, the night manager keeps coming in mornings; now what can that mean? The cook says things like, 'Be careful with those plates, honey; that's hot stuff'—and he's old enough to be my father! The bus boy cleans my tables before everyone else's and once a day, the cashier hollers, 'I'm getting off soon! Need a hand, here.' I always, I mean *always*, feel them checking me out. I don't know where to turn. I never do."

"I'd be happy to come by and watch over you," said Jollie. "If any of those gorillas bothers you again, it'll be the last time, I can promise you that. I was a star athlete. Football, baseball—"

"That would be grand, Jollie," said Peppy, thinking how Jud Roy would have approved of the word *grand*. "I'd feel a lot safer knowing you were there." She was getting excited thinking about how jealous Jud Roy would get if she flirted with Jollie. "Maybe I could even sneak you some free pancakes," she suggested.

"Ah! My favorite dish," said Jollie. He reached for her hand, but she turned away, and began applying lipstick.

"I start work at eight in the morning," she said over her shoulder. Jollie admired her freshly painted mouth.

Peppy began sneaking pancakes to Jollie. She never offered free pancakes to Jud Roy, and it made him crazy with jealousy. Peppy enjoyed torturing him because it turned her on, but the professor was not sophisticated enough to understand the logic in this and thought she was interested in Jollie. Meanwhile, Jollie was sure he would soon win the beautiful woman over.

He liked to interrupt the class to thank Peppy for the pancakes.

"Peppy, I want to thank you for the extra whipped cream on those strawberry sundae pancakes you made me this morning!" he announced once while a woman tried to read her short story, "Olive Garden—the Very First Time."

Whenever Jollie thanked Peppy for the pancakes, Jud Roy took to telling Jollie to shut up, and Jollie took to thanking Peppy for the pancakes more often.

"Peppy, my dear, you are a perfect peach, just like the ripe ones that graced my breakfast yesterday," said Jollie. "I swear I never saw such lovely, rosy peaches. They begged for syrup."

"Shut up, Jollie," said Jud Roy.

The next class, Jollie leaned toward Peppy with moon cow eyes.

"Peppy, how wonderful are the mornings watching you serve me." He thought that was a particularly good line.

"Well, waiting on the customers, even the ones that don't pay is part of my job," Peppy smiled.

Jud Roy gritted his teeth. "Jollie, that you can't pay for a cheap stack of pancakes is nothing to be proud of," he sneered.

Jollie's comments got worse. "Peppy, when you bent over to pick up that fork this morning...allow me to say that I would crawl at your feet to look up your dress again."

Peppy flipped her hair, and crossed and uncrossed her legs.

Jud Roy knew that if he was going to make time with Peppy, he had to make a move before Jollie did. The professor began asking that she stay after class, which delighted her and pissed off Jollie.

"Excuse me, Peppy. I would like to see you again after class. It's very important—it may impact your entire future."

"Of course." Peppy fluttered her eyelashes and tried to look innocent.

Jud Roy began with his usual bullshit flattery.

"Peppy, I've been thinking long and hard about your essay "Scandinavia." Such sensitivity! Such pathos! I don't wonder you won the creative writing award in high school. What I can't understand is why you're not published. We really must start your tutoring sessions. No charge."

Peppy said, "Do you really mean it, Jud Roy? Do you really see me as more than just a pretty face? Do I really have talent? "

"Peppy, my professional opinion is that your writing is not only publishable, it is best-seller material."

"No!" Peppy gasped. "Surely it can't be as good as that." She pressed her breasts in disbelief.

"Oh, yes. As good as that, and more," said Jud Roy, smiling.

"I would love for you to be my tutor, Jud Roy," Peppy said breathlessly.

"Now that we have established a business relationship, please call me Professor Lebowitz. To learn from a superior, one must show respect."

"Yes, Professor Lebowitz." Peppy's toes curled inside her high-heeled shoes.

"We should begin our tutoring sessions immediately. Maybe we could go somewhere for a cheeseburger and discuss your future. There's a wonderful bistro, Burgers and Booze, a short mile from my place."

"Do they have specialty drinks?" Peppy asked.

"Of course," Jud Roy lied.

Peppy smiled. "I've never gone out with one of my teachers before. It sounds a little dangerous. But I really, really like you."

"Shall I pick you up tomorrow, around seven? It's Saturday, so there shouldn't be much traffic."

"Sometimes a Saturday means more traffic," Peppy reminded him.

"Only when there's a baseball game," Jud Roy said.

"No, no, I go out a lot on Saturday nights and there's always traffic," Peppy insisted.

Jud Roy corrected her. "No, traffic's OK. It's parking that's the problem."

"Parking's always a problem, especially," said Peppy. "There are no lots."

"I don't need any damn lot—I can parallel park like that!" Jud Roy snapped his fingers in her face.

"I love a man who can parallel park. But can you find a space?" challenged Peppy.

"Oh, I can find a space. I always find a space."

Peppy put her hands on her hips. "No way—everyone's out on Saturdays and most of them are driving around looking for a place to park—don't you ever go anywhere?"

"Oh, I go somewhere. I'm always going somewhere if I'm not already there. Oh, yes. And you needn't take that high tone with me, missy. The Parking God and I have a special relationship."

"And just why should the Parking God bother with you?" Peppy asked.

Jud Roy snapped back, "Why should he bother with me? I'll tell you why. It's like this—whenever I kill a fly or a spider or a rat, I say, 'I sacrifice this rat to you, Great Parking God,' and he takes care of me."

"And it works?" Peppy considered.

"Of course it does," said Jud Roy kindly, wondering if he was going to get any after all. "So I'll pick you up at seven?"

"Oh, yes—at seven."

"I've enjoyed our conversation. Immensely," Jud said, suddenly all politeness.

"Yeah, me too—I mean, yes, I also, Professor Lebowitz." Peppy took his hand briefly and left.

"See you tonight…Burgers and Booze is on First and Date Streets," said Jud Roy.

Peppy interrupted. "I'll be there. I have to get to my writing group now, Professor Lebowitz. They'll be waiting for me."

Now Jollie would be jealous of Jud Roy. Peppy could bounce her attentions between the two of them. Her mission accomplished, she abruptly told Jollie that she had to stop giving him free pancakes—Jollie was mad. The loss of his pancake privileges could only mean that Peppy had agreed to go out with Jud Roy Lebowitz.

CHAPTER 16

Burgers and Booze

● ● ●

SATURDAY NIGHTS, BURGERS AND BOOZE was crowded, cheesy, and hot. The burgers hissed and spit on a flatiron grill, and the fries splattered beef-scented oil. Jud Roy and Peppy sat at an awkward, tilted table with a red-checked plastic tablecloth and a wine bottle that spouted a lopsided candle and hardened wax.

Jud Roy went to the bar and returned with a pitcher of beer. "They're all out of the well drinks. It happens a lot during happy hour. Next time, we'll make a reservation."

The food was delicious. Sloppy, drippy hamburgers, huge portions of fries with that perfect crisp, and no vegetables except for the lettuce, tomato, pickle, and raw onion. Oh—and a chocolate shake served in the ice-cold silver container they'd mixed the shake in. It was the great American meal, fit for a shameless king who did not fear public opinion. Jud Roy and Peppy held hands over the sticky table. They discussed the fine parking space Jud Roy had found and how much they both disliked Jollie. At the end of the date, Jud Roy took Peppy to his apartment.

Jud Roy's apartment was on the top floor of an ancient building that had survived two earthquakes. He'd lived there for ten years. The apartments were stacked up around a tall, empty space that opened to the sky. If there were a fire, the whole building would become a chimney that sucked the fire to the top. Within minutes, the fire would engulf the entire building in flames, but it had not happened, which was a testament to blind chance. The rest of the apartment was a tiny bathroom and a bedroom, which was also the kitchen.

"I was so afraid!" Peppy's voice shook with staggering drama, and she put her arms around Jud Roy. "So afraid. What a terrifying ordeal! Men are such animals, and yet—they must be to be men. One never knows what one will ask one to do. What a man wants to do may not even exist on the Internet. Believe me; I know. One must be strong. If one is to play the game." The beautiful woman hid her face in his chest.

"By your artistic repetition of the word *one*, I feel your creativity and sensitivity. You can be safe with me, Peppy. You can trust me to listen. Tell me, Peppy. Tell me all the things that a man ever did to you. I will not be shocked, no matter how deviant or disgusting the tale," said Jud Roy. Rainbow-colored smears from Peppy's makeup embellished his shirt.

Peppy said nothing, only fell into Jud Roy's arms and sobbed.

The professor led Peppy to his bed and lay down to comfort her. She comforted him in turn. They comforted one another until the sun rose. Afterward, Jud Roy decided to join the Three Musketeers. He knew where they met, and with the exception of Jollie, he was sure that they would welcome him. Peppy was his now, so Jollie didn't matter.

"Oh, hell," Jollie muttered, and then wiped his face with a bit of cloud. "After all these years, I still love that girl."

CHAPTER 17

Second Reading

● ● ●

MEANWHILE, THE CLASS FOLLOWED THE same format they did the first day the students had read. The students brought in something to read. Each reading ended with brief comments nobody cared about. By the time all sixteen students had read, it was time to go.

A handsome young man went first with a limerick:

You Wanna Piece of Me?

I like to drink bourbon and whiskey
When I drink, my behavior gets risky.
For I drink with a style
That some call hostile,
But that I call refreshingly frisky.

"Class?" asked Jud Roy.

Nobody said anything.

A librarian-dressed middle-aged woman also read a limerick:

Why I Have No Friends

The problem with my indigestion
is its singular mode of expression,
for I swell with a gas

that explodes out my ass,
and it cannot be done with discretion.

"Comments?" asked Jud Roy.

There were none.

A pig-nosed man read a short story entitled "Blondes Are Better in Bed."

When I was a young lad of sixteen years, I discovered that blondes are better in bed because they are always more beautiful than any other women. I have never had sex with a brunette or, God forbid, a red-haired woman. I would rather lie back in my bed and think about blondes, and I believe most men feel the same way. Just last week, I paid a blonde to do a lap dance. It was excellent, and I am seeing her tonight, even though I had to borrow money to do it.

"Class?" Jud Roy asked.

Peppy could hardly wait. "Your very interesting paper makes me wonder if you ever had a woman you didn't have to pay for."

Leslie explained, "It's not about a real woman. It's a story with a message. The message is, Beware a Pale Horse."

Peppy said, "Except that it's, Beware a Pale Blonde. I couldn't agree more. The Scandinavians are all blond and certainly not to be trusted. Why, they don't even have a president."

Leslie made no reply.

"I appreciate your input, Peppy." Jud Roy said importantly. "I am sure that if Scandinavia had a president, he would smell of fish. Class is over."

"Mr. Lebowitz!" the high-school dropout called out. "I haven't read yet!"

"We really don't care," said Jud Roy. Why don't you go work at McDarnold's with the rest of the losers?"

Leslie objected to Jud Roy's comment. "I hardly think that's fair," she said. "McDarnold's is one of the greatest success stories in the world. While a person may start lower than low vis-à-vis the pay scale, with dedication and hard work, he or she may develop the skills to start their own business and make a good, even a substantial living."

"Yeah, thanks, Leslie. But I have a feeling that McDarnold's may soon be over. Fast food is out. It's all about gluten-free," said Jud Roy. "That's where the money is."

A man whom Leslie had recognized on the first day of class as the engineer, who so admired her "Pyramids of Giza" fruit display at Ye Olde Grocery, joined the discussion.

"You are quite right, sir." He addressed Jud Roy. "And gluten-free is here to stay. Regarding McDarnold's however, I have invented a gluten-free hamburger patty made from oatmeal that has been chemically altered to taste like beef. By selling my altered oatmeal patty to McDarnold's as a gluten-free option, I also avoid taxes and government regulations, because gluten-free foods are classified as medicinal kindness."

The woman wearing a red dress that fit like a wiener-skin spoke up. "Gluten-free hamburgers, do you say? I believe I read something about that somewhere some time ago in a some article in a paper whose name I don't remember."

"I missed that particular article, but the idea of including gluten-free options in the fast food industry is a guaranteed win. The market will explode! That means, ladies," the man explained to the women, "the stock market, not the grocery store. I'm a businessman, so I know all about these things. Yes, I'm a businessman." He nodded and smiled at the ladies who were not listening but nodded back in assent.

"Weren't you an engineer in Livermore?" asked Leslie suspiciously.

"So I was!" said the man. "I am also a lawyer, a physician, and an opera singer." He winked at Leslie. She was glad her bomb shelter was well hidden.

Jud Roy cut the discussion short by announcing, "Well done, everyone," and hurrying out to dab on fresh Old Spat de Toilet for Peppy, whom he always tried to sit with at the meetings with the Three Musketeers.

Jollie rushed out after him. He also looked forward to sitting next to Peppy at the meetings. Instead of Old Spat, he dabbed Poor Him. Jud Roy and Peppy were now dating regularly, but Jollie still tried. It was difficult, however, to compete with Jud Roy, what with the professor's status and salary. What Jollie didn't know was that the miserly salary of a part-time instructor at an adult-education school came to very little. As for Peppy, she'd grown up poor, and she was too enthralled with Jud Roy's title and position to notice that he was always broke.

CHAPTER 18

The Allmart Greeter

● ● ●

BECAUSE JUD ROY COULD NOT afford to take Peppy to expensive places like amusement parks or the Dead Lobster, he found cheaper entertainment. Bowling was good. They were regulars at the Hoegaarden and Burgers and Booze. One of their favorite things to do was to go to Allmart because it was near both their apartments and they could always find something they could afford to buy. The only downside was the Allmart greeter.

"Welcome to Allmart," said Jollie.

Jollie's unemployment benefits had run out, and he'd been forced to take a job at Allmart. His interview had been brief.

"Why do you think you are qualified to perform the important position of Allmart greeter?" asked the head manager, Mr. Cheese.

Jollie threw his head back and snorted a laugh. "If I told you my plans, you'd never believe it. I'm a very ambitious person." He smoothed his red Hermes tie.

"Why did you leave your last employment, Mr. Itch?"

"Inch," Jollie corrected him. "My name is Inch. Why did I leave? There was too little interaction with people. I'm a real friendly guy, the kind of guy who gets along with everybody. I'm a cocktail-party kind of guy. Nearly every night, but I never get tired. It's how I work; it's how I play. Haw! WWW had to hire five people to replace me."

"WWW?"

"The Wonderful World of Wicker," Jollie said. "I worked for nine, er, nineteen years for the Wonderful World of Wicker, biggest wicker-basket company in the world. I mean, serious international."

"Thank you, Mr. Itch. We'll be in touch."

"Inch. Jollie Inch. The Inches have quite a Wild West history. Evil men accused my great-great-great uncle of horse thievery and then hung him, but God exonerated him when the rope broke. I'm afraid I need to know about the job immediately. There are several headhunters after me."

"Did he live?"

"Who?"

"Your grand—uh, whatever, your relative's uncle."

"No, it was too late. An honest man died that day."

"OK—you're hired. Welcome to Allmart. You start tomorrow, eight in the morning, sharp."

Mr. Cheese sighed. They hadn't had a greeter in months. People didn't seem to want them anymore.

"I had quite a résumé by that time," Jollie said to himself. He made a snowball from cloud fluff and threw it at Mr. Cheese.

Every Saturday afternoon, Jud Roy and Peppy went to Allmart for beer and ice cream. Because he hated seeing Jud Roy with Peppy, Jollie usually denied them their welcome. One gray afternoon, however, Peppy was looking particularly fetching, and Jollie could not resist speaking to her.

"Why Peppy—you're looking lovely today. Allow me to extend a warm welcome to Allmart. Oh—Jud Roy again. My condolences Peppy, my dear."

"There's some people over there that need welcoming," Jud Roy said and tried to walk on, but Peppy held back.

She flipped her hair and smiled at Jollie. That would make Jud Roy, mad and she liked making Jud Roy mad, especially on Saturday nights, when she didn't have to get up to go to work the next day.

Jollie stared at Peppy. She was as beautiful as a Barbie doll. He wondered if she had breast implants. He had never felt breast implants before.

"Say, Peppy—have you ever seen the 'No Access to the Public' section of Allmart? It's really quite interesting. I could give you a tour. You never saw so many boxes."

Peppy wiggled and widened her eyes. She pretended to love the idea.

"I guess I'll see you at class Wednesday," said Jud Roy, and he guided Peppy out of the store. "We'll get our beer and ice cream at the liquor store, where it costs more but they don't welcome you."

"Good-bye Jollie," said Peppy, smiling.

"Good-bye Beautiful," said Jollie from the cloud.

After walking Peppy home, Jud Roy returned to Allmart to confront Jollie.

"Welcome to Allmart. We've got more plastic crap than anyone," Jollie said. "Oh—it's you again."

Jud Roy stood as tall as he was able. "Jollie—as your professor and mentor, I must inform you that being seen with a woman like Peppy is certain to damage the reputation of a serious writer like yourself, a man with a future, a man with talent plus. I'm telling you as a professional—a woman like Peppy—why, readers would steer clear of whatever you write, you could lose it all, all, you understand, everything you've worked for. I know you will do the right thing."

"Sure, sure," said Jollie. "Don't worry about me. I get all the tail I want working here at Allmart. Women going in and out, day and night, night and day. Whenever a guy tells me he can't find a woman, I tell him, 'Come to Allmart. That's where all the women are.' And that's the truth."

"Just stay away from her, Jollie. For your own sake—if you persist, I will be obliged to report your behavior to your manager. For your own good, you understand. For the good of your future public."

"Yeah, well, I guess you don't have to worry about being seen with a loose woman since you're a talentless nitwit. Welcome to Allmart."

"Maybe I'll just speak to your supervisor right now!"

"There he is..." Jollie pointed to Mr. Stroganoff, a huge ex-wrestler who had broken his leg tripping over an emotional-support dachshund that had wandered between Mr. Stroganoff's legs. The accident left Mr.

Stroganoff with a permanent limp. He'd had to give up wrestling and take a janitor's job at Allmart. The former smiling playboy was now an angry gimp who scowled.

The professor took one look at Mr. Stroganoff, and decided to give Jollie another chance. Perhaps his threat to complain would be enough to end Jollie's interest in Peppy.

But Jollie would not leave the beautiful woman alone. Every Saturday, when Peppy and Jud Roy came in to Allmart to buy beer and ice cream, he stared boldly at Peppy. Now, he stared from the cloud, but he was just as bold.

CHAPTER 19

The Three Musketeers Struggle Along

● ● ●

PEPPY, LESLIE, AND DINO, THE original Three Musketeers, had gotten along semi well, but with the two men, the meetings escalated into foul language and anger. Jollie never tired of making suggestions to change the name of the group.

"How about something masculine—The Five Wrestling Billy Goats."

Jollie always laughed so hard when he heard himself say that, that he fell backward into the cloud. It was a stupid joke, really, but there was nobody there to remind him.

"How about One Foot, Five Perfect Toes?" Jud Roy spit back. "Or why don't you join another group and write a limerick entitled 'There Once Was a Greeter from Allmart?'"

Jollie couldn't think of anything to say. Jud Roy smirked because he had won. The women sniped about pizza toppings. They'd planned to have dinner together that night.

It hadn't started out that way. By the time Jud Roy joined the group, the Three Musketeers had set specific rules for their meetings, rules that were supposed to keep things civilized. Members would take turns reading first. After each one finished, everyone discussed the reader's work. All comments had to be positive. Sometimes they ran out of words—things like, "That was amazing," "You've improved so much," and "Wow" quickly became old and stale.

Initially, the three women correctly believed that the breakdown in order was the men's fault. Now, everyone was breaking the rules. Members came and went whenever they wanted to. Most of the comments were negative, and the men were sparring all the time. Jollie would interrupt the others by shouting things like, "Now that's an essay!" or "It made me want to cry." Between comments, Dino meditated, Peppy applied and reapplied makeup, and Leslie sat quietly, thinking about her peaceful room in the bomb shelter.

"Thank God your memoir ended when it did. Fortunately, it won't be hard to forget." (Jud Roy to Leslie.)

"Geez, you must be so embarrassed. I'd hide my face if I wrote that." (Leslie to Jud Roy.)

"When you started reading, I thought it was stupid, sexy, and weird. When you finished reading, I knew it was only stupid and weird." (Peppy to Dino.)

"That's supposed to be a poem? A poem has to follow rules! It has to rhyme! Otherwise, it's just a bunch of words." (Mr. Bottomly, who had stopped in to look at Peppy, to Jud Roy.)

"Hurry up, so I can read!" (Jollie to everyone).

Jollie was selectively rotten. He always saved the worst of his degrading comments for Jud Roy. A sonnet that Jud Roy had worked on all night entitled "Can a Woman Be True?" inspired the remark, "What a stink pile!"

Jud Roy was getting angrier and angrier. The professor decided that he would brave the muscle-bound Mr. Stroganoff and get Jollie fired. When he walked into Allmart the next day, Jollie was busily greeting customers.

"Welcome, ma'am—welcome to Allmart. Ah, what a cute little monkey," he said, smiling at the child in the cart. "Welcome to All—oh, it's you again."

"I want to speak to a manager," Jud Roy demanded. He glanced around for Mr. Stroganoff, and was relieved not to see him. "Any manager," he said fiercely.

"All of our managers are very busy—you'll have to wait, probably a long, long time," warned Jollie.

"I'll wait," snapped Jud Roy. He loitered about the entrance, happily picking out the funny-looking people and delighting in their misery.

Fifty minutes later, a thin, nervous man with a buzzard head and a crooked neck showed up. "A customer wishes to see me?" he asked Jollie. "That's him," Jollie said, and pointed to Jud Roy.

The thin man approached Jud Roy. "I am Mr. Pimpernel, the manager. May I help you, sir?" The man had an odd habit of bobbing his head up and down to the rhythm of his speech. Safety pins sparkled from the inside of his sports coat.

"My name is Professor Jud Roy Lebowitz. It's about your Allmart greeter. He made me feel unwelcome when I came in today. I was going to spend a lot of money, but now I'm taking my business to To-Get, even though their prices are higher."

"We here at Allmart do not worry about substandard stores like To-Get." (And here the buzzard head snorted.) "We have every confidence that our connections with third-world countries bring our customers the very best prices."

Jud Roy raised his voice so that others could hear.

"While it is true that Allmart's low prices are legendary, that is not the issue. That greeter is a menace to society. He told me the other day, 'Velkommen to Allmart,' an obvious insult to my Jewish heritage."

"You asshole!" shouted Jollie, who crouched behind a shopping cart, where he could get closer without being noticed and hear the conversation better.

A woman walked in and he jumped up and startled her. "Welcome to Allmart," Jollie piped, and gave her a stiff smile.

"My work here is done," said Jud Roy, and he walked out, leaving buzzard head to apologize to Allmart customers who had been injured by Jollie's foul language.

Mr. Pimpernel knew that Jollie was the worst greeter in the history of Allmart, but to fire someone involved so many meetings and so much paperwork, by the time it was done, the employee had usually either moved on or died. Nonetheless, Mr. Pimpernel dutifully started the hellish process then gave up after a week. People didn't shop at Allmart for the greeters anyway; they shopped at Allmart because it was a cheap hobby.

Jud Roy was sure that his remark about his Jewish heritage would get Jollie fired. He called Peppy as soon as he got home. "He's done— he's washed up. You should have seen his supervisor. A big guy, about six foot three, in a pinstripe suit. This guy, he comes out and yells, 'You're fired!' right there in front of everyone. Jollie starts begging this guy not to fire him. The guy loses it, grabs him by the hair, and throws him out of the store! Jollie actually started to cry."

"Well, that *is* interesting," Peppy said. "So what was the name of his supervisor? Maybe I should stop by and talk to him about Jollie too." Jud Roy's professor status was wearing off. Peppy tired of men quickly.

Jud Roy was silent.

"So what was the Allmart supervisor's name?" Peppy asked again. "Maybe I should go and complain that Jollie sexually harassed me—he has, you know. Lots of times. Just like that bus boy at Pancake Heaven. Now, the cook's started. He said, just the other day, 'Your hotcakes are up!' and the pancakes weren't even ready. Men are all the same. Even the nice ones are exactly like the others."

"Great," said Jud Roy. He hung up without saying good-bye.

Meanwhile, the Three Musketeer's meetings continued to deteriorate. Jollie was especially vocal. One evening, Leslie struggled for fifteen minutes to read her essay entitled "Scandinavia Is Not a Country."

"Scandinavia Is Not a Country," she began.

Jollie lounged against the side wall. "What the hell else could it be?" he shouted. He grinned at the rest of the group.

Leslie went on. "Scandinavia is a province in Northern Europe composed of Sweden, Denmark, Norway, and some say Finland."

"Hey, Leslie—you know how bad you'd look in wooden shoes? Better than you look regular ones." Jollie was feeling particularly witty that day.

Leslie continued.

"The most important thing to know about Scandinavia is that there is almost nothing to do there, so the Scandinavian people spend most of their time hiking in the beautiful countryside and drinking alcohol. Scandinavia has the healthiest alcoholics in the world. Helge von Koch, father of the van Koch of triangle snowflake fame, was from Sweden and is the acknowledged hero of all of the countries that make up Scandinavia, although most people have never heard of him and probably never will."

"Indeed?" said Jud Roy, yawning.

"Ha! Go back to school, dingbat!" sneered Jollie. The others laughed.

Leslie sat down and mouthed a silent "Fuck You".

Jollie watched from the cloud. He had not noticed her rubbing her hands at the time, but he'd seen the video too many times now to not notice. It bothered him. *I wonder why she was so obsessed with Scandinavia,* he asked himself.

Peppy went next. "It's my turn to go now. I know I read it in class, but I feel especially proud of my work today. Here, once more, is my parody entitled 'My Love Is Like a Dead, Dead Rose' based on the original poem by William Shakespeare."

Leslie spoke up. "Shakespeare didn't write that—it was Ro—"

"I love Shakespeare," Jud Roy said, interrupting. "What thou art but a window sill?" he crooned.

"Yes," agreed Peppy. "'My Love Is Like a Dead, Dead Rose' was Shakespeare's way of saying that love is a thorny business. Shakespeare was a very romantic man, although domineering and possessive, as illustrated in his greatest work, *The Taming with the Shoe.*"

"Can you just get on with it, so I can read?" As usual, Jollie was getting impatient.

Peppy flipped him off and read.

My Love is Like a Dead, Dead Rose

O, my love is like a dead, dead rose,
He takes me to sawdust saloons.

I'm too good for him because he's poor.
I want my oil tycoon.

Jud Roy frowned. "I would have expected better from you, Peppy."
"You got no business expecting anything from her!" hollered Jollie. He gazed at Peppy and his voice melted to a smooth chocolate tone. "Your poem moved me, Peppy darling. In a way I would blush to admit."

Jud Roy threw an eraser at him but hit Dino instead.

Dino looked down at the rectangular imprint of chalk across her breasts. "I sense, deep within my nether regions, an aura of negativity. Perhaps something on the topic of ethereal existence will bring an atmosphere of calm," she suggested, and stood up to read.

Up above, Jollie imagined laying his head against the imprint of the chalk from the eraser.

The Subway

Steel bindings encase the world like a corset, people forever ride, back and forth, and forth and back, on the forbidden tracks that no one dares look at, for to touch a single rail is death.
Where will you be when the tracks give out? In a carpool, there is warmth and shared lives. In a subway, there are no faces.
Between friends, weather should not be a topic of conversation.

Dino smiled and sat down.

Peppy was impressed. "It's supposed to be sexy, right? I mean, that part about the steel corset?" Peppy sighed.

Jud Roy clapped his hands. "Hear, hear! I thought as much. Women can't write enough about sex. Men always write too much. Thank you, Dino. Now, I believe it's my turn to read." Jud Roy cleared his throat. "Now here's something you'll really enjoy."

The Man, The Myth, The Legend

He knows what women want. Sawdust, haystacks, mud, and sand. A man must be a man. A tuxedo-dressed fop with a silk handkerchief and credit cards can buy things, but he's a loser in the sack. Good sex is better than haute cuisine, and more difficult to find. Show your manhood by wearing a classic cologne—Old Spat has been winning women's hearts for years. Old Spat—guaranteed to make women crazy. Not for human consumption. May be fatal to animals and young children.

Nobody commented.

Jollie stood in front of the class to read. The other members of the group always read from their chairs, but Jollie still liked to stand and make sure everyone was watching him.

He always began by gargling water and spitting into a paper cup.

"Silence! I am about to read the story I read in class today. As you know, the class was so enthralled that when I finished, they dared not speak."

Peppy didn't like to share the spotlight. "Jollie, please—my essay last week, 'Sexual Oddities, Autobiography of a Freak' kicked your ass."

Jollie softened his temper. "Only a lady like yourself could charm with such words," he said, looking at her breasts. Peppy hadn't taken him up on his offer to give her a tour of Allmart, but Jollie still hoped.

"You couldn't make a babe with tits like that to save your life! She's the heartthrob of Scandinavia!" sneered Jud Roy.

"Her breasts are perfect mounds of marshmallow heaven," Jollie announced and flourished his paper toward her ample bosom. "And I am sure all of Scandinavia would agree." He tried to give her a smoldering look that came off as a dead stare.

Jud Roy grabbed Peppy's hand, and then remembered how she'd talked about wanting to meet Jollie's supervisor. Jud Roy dropped her hand, a thing Jollie noted and silently cheered. Peppy adjusted her bra, and enjoyed the men's attention.

Leslie tried again, "You know, Scandinavia really isn't a country."

"Leslie, you are such an idiot," Peppy snapped.

Leslie silently thought "Bitch" and pictured Peppy with a shaved head.

"Don't listen to her, Peppy," said Jollie. "I would love to hear you read about your trip to Scandinavia again." Peppy sighed deeply and arched her back. She found it hard to resist any man's compliments, and Jud Roy was proving to be a disappointment.

Jud Roy hated hearing Jollie and Peppy's sexually charged repartee. "Silence, please! You are all rude, brash, and overbearing."

Everyone settled down. Better to get it over with.

"Uh—hem! 'Secret Agent in a Fast Car with a Naked Woman,'" Jollie announced.

Secret Agent in a Fast Car with a Naked Woman

A secret agent, whose name cannot be disclosed for his protection, was speeding along at two hundred miles an hour on a winding country road, when a naked woman in a convertible stood up and waved at him. 'Good God!' the secret agent said. 'That woman's not wearing a seatbelt!' He pulled her over, handcuffed her, and put her in the car. The naked woman fell in love with him and wouldn't leave him alone, so he finally shot her with a Glock-19, semiautomatic because he was a secret agent and he could do it. A helicopter from Channel 7 flew over to report the incident, and he shot it down with a high-energy laser gun because he was a secret agent and he could do it. On his way home, a traffic-enforcement camera took a picture of him running a red light, so he shot it with a Sig Saur, P226, semiautomatic because he could do it. At the end of his career, he got the Medal of Honor and a ticker tape parade in a secret ceremony because he was a secret agent, and he had to hide his identity. There were lots of women there, and they all wanted him, but he couldn't give them his name or his phone number because he would have to kill him them then too. Nobody every investigated the shootings, and nobody cared. Instead of putting him in jail, they made a movie about him.

"I knew a real secret agent, once," said Peppy. "I went out with one. You just made up yours."

Leslie sketched in her notebook, Peppy applied lipstick, Jud Roy watched Peppy applying lipstick, and Dino prayed gratitude over a fish stick she had brought to snack on. When Jollie finished, Dino offered him the fish stick.

"Jollie Inch, share with me my gift of life," she said.

"Weirdo," Jollie answered and slapped it out of her hand. It fell to the floor, and he mashed it into the carpet with his foot.

"I hate Jollie," whispered Dino to Peppy. "I hate his essence. I hate Leslie too. And there *is* a country called Scandinavia. I've been there in a dream."

Jollie overheard. "With regard to me, what you call hate, I call jealousy. But I hate Leslie too," he said.

Leslie lost it enough to shoot back, "Arrogant fool! One day, you'll realize you're an idiot who doesn't have the sense to be embarrassed!" She quietly muttered foul words to herself.

"I've never been embarrassed in life!" countered Jollie.

"I love a man who can't be embarrassed," murmured Peppy. "Why don't you just admit you're wrong about Scandinavia?" she asked Leslie.

Leslie folded her hands in front of her mouth. "Go to hell," she whispered into her hands.

Jud Roy was tired of the bickering. "I'm tired of this bickering," he said in no uncertain terms.

They all settled down. Jud Roy was, after all, the teacher. But for how long? The following day, he had a meeting with Mr. Bottomly. He didn't know why Mr. Bottomly wanted to see him, but it couldn't be good.

CHAPTER 20

Problem

● ● ●

JUD ROY WAS USED TO sleeping in late. When the alarm went off, he fell out of bed. "Goddamnit!" he yelled and rubbed a banged knee.

Jud Roy put on his green plaid sports coat and headed out to his car. He drove erratically and worried himself through two traffic lights and a stop sign. He arrived at Mr. Bottomly's office two minutes late.

Mr. Bottomly's office door seemed larger than Jud Roy remembered. Jud Roy knocked. "Come in, Mr. Lebowitz." Mr. Bottomly's pristine office was unchanged.

"Good morning, sir," said Jud Roy. He stood attentively in front of Mr. Bottomly's desk, hands folded in front of him, his body stiff.

Although Mr. Bottomly sat at his desk, he did not ask Jud Roy to sit down. Mr. Bottomly looked at his watch and frowned. He struggled to calm his crooked eye and, for a few seconds, managed to steady both eyes on Jud Roy. Jud Roy knew he could not keep it up and focused on the wall behind Mr. Bottomly.

"Professor Lebowitz," Mr. Bottomly said, "over the last two years, we have received several letters of complaint—indeed, sir, *several* letters of complaint about the creative writing class—*your* class, Mr. Professor Lebowitz. We at Millard Fillmore Elementary-Adult Education take great pride in offering quality, I say, *quality* education to both children and adults. It appears that, I should say it *seems* to appear, that you have not been providing that. Failure is not an option here at Millard Fillmore. Nor should it be at any American educational institution, although I am ashamed to say that our schools are not what they used to be. However, I should mention our children of the Jewish faith do not seem to have any problems meeting our high academic standards. My opinion is that it is a result of their mothers staying at home instead of gallivanting around in some shameless workplace."

Jud Roy raised his hands and drew back. His eyebrows shot up and his mouth and eyes made three large circles.

"Indeed? I am all astonishment, Mr. Bottomly. I cannot anticipate the abilities of the students who sign up for my class. This quarter, however, I have four very talented students whom I am certain will reflect my dedication and hard work in teaching at Millard. By the way, was Millard Fillmore a relative of yours? You bear a distinct resemblance to a sketch of the former president that I saw on the Internet. Except for the eye, of cour—except for the color of the eyes."

The superintendent ignored his question and went on. "Four talented students, you say? You say four?" he said, tapping a pencil on the desk. "It might be the solution to a problem—you know, solutions are what make men great. Not so much women. Solving problems makes them less attractive. The PTA meetings have become boring, painfully so, and membership is dropping off. There is a PTA meeting scheduled in a month—in one month, mind you. I had the idea that the meeting could conclude with some kind of entertainment—a demonstration of what we do here at Millard. Perhaps you could bring your four best students and have them read aloud. Of course, having them simply read aloud is a little dull, tedious if you will, and not very interesting."

"Adults providing entertainment at the PTA? Wouldn't you want children?" Jud Roy asked.

Mr. Bottomly's mouth stretched into a harsh, thin line. "The PTA is sick of children reciting the alphabet and singing 'Itsy Bitsy Spider.' This is, after all, a PTA meeting, I mean to say, a meeting of the Parent-Teacher Association, which is an association for both parents and teachers, adult parents and teachers, I should say. I don't know any parent or teacher who wants to spend *more* time with children. We have a mature audience, we need mature entertainment, something that will entertain, that will show parents that the PTA can be fun. By the way, who's that red-haired woman with the unusually large breasts I keep seeing you with?"

Now Jud Roy ignored Mr. Bottomly's question. "What about a play? My four best students could both write and perform it for the PTA. I'm sure it would be very entertaining and a credit to the school. How would that be?"

"An appropriate suggestion." Mr. Bottomly secretly loved the idea. "A play, you say? The school board will be most pleased. I'll make up flyers to mail with the notices about the PTA meeting. My assistant, Ms. Jenkins will design them. Something like, 'In addition to the meeting, an exclusive showing of a play, written, directed, and performed by four of the most talented students ever,' um—what are the names of the students?"

"Peppy Zipline, Leslie Tomatiny, Dino Quiet Room, and Jollie Inch."

"Jollie Itch?"

"Inch. Jollie *I-N-C-H*."

"Who's this Peppy Zipline? Seems I've heard her name before."

"I can't imagine where. She's one of the four students I mentioned. Pretty, but in an ordinary kind of a way." Jud Roy wrote the four names on the back of a pizza coupon he had in his pocket and handed the coupon to Mr. Bottomly.

The superintendent looked at the coupon. He seemed surprised. "Hi-Ho Pizza—great place. I approve of pizza, so long as it is made the American way, with plenty of meat and cheese. I especially like the young women pizza delivery boys. Well, thank you, Mr. Roy, er, Lebowitz. The meeting is in one month. Specifically 17 March—March, the seventeenth of this year, mind you. That's three, one, seven, two thousand and fifteen. We start at six and end at eight. You will begin your show at nineteen hundred—excuse me, old habit—you will begin at seven thirty at night."

"I look forward to it. Such a wonderful opportunity—I'm sure my students will be delighted," said Jud Roy. Jud Roy walked out of the office, and Mr. Bottomly turned on a favorite documentary, *Undervalued Presidential Speeches*.

As soon as Jud Roy turned the corner, Jollie snuck out from behind an oleander bush and knocked on the superintendent's door. Mr. Bottomly jumped up and shut off the TV.

"Uh-hem! Come in."

Jollie did so. Mr. Bottomly was sitting at his desk, his ear to the phone. He nodded busily and frowned. The phone rang in Mr. Bottomly's ear, and he hung it up.

Mr. Bottomly asked, "Yes? Can I do something for you—I mean, what can I do for your assistance? State your business, sir; I'm a busy man. Ordinarily, people make appointments. I should note that you did not." He wrote something down on a piece of paper.

Jollie cleared his throat. "Hem! My apologies, Mr. Bottomly. I'm not sure if you recognize me. I'm a new student this semester. My name is Jollie Inch, and I'm enrolled in Jud Roy's creative writing class."

"Indeed? If you are a student, you should be addressing me as Superintendent. What a coincidence that you are studying creative writing. Professor Jud Roy was just here. He and I were discussing a very interesting project for his class to participate, er, take place in—I mean to say, perform." His eye swam left, and then right, and then bounced toward the ceiling.

Jollie bobbed his head to catch the impossible eye. He gave up and focused on a missing button on Mr. Bottomly's shirt.

"A new project, Superintendent Bottomly? I'm surprised that Professor Lebowitz did not discuss it with me. Modesty aside, I am his top student—he has told me so many times. Doubtless, I will figure substantially in the new project."

"Professor Jud Roy informs me that some of the students this year are very talented. Normally, I disapprove of adults engaging in such frivolity, but we must entertain the PTA, or so says the school board."

"I confess, Superintendent Bottomly, that there are a few students that stand out from the rest. In fact, we belong to an exclusive writing group that meets after school. They are however beginners to the craft. They probably wrote something in school years ago and were praised by an ignorant teacher. One of them told me she won the creative writing award in high school. I, on the other hand, have been writing for years to much acclaim. Much acclaim." Jollie smirked and rolled his eyes. "Oh, yes—I wrote my autobiography when I was only five years old. But that is not why

I am here. I have some serious concerns about Jud Roy and his outrageous behavior toward one of his female students."

"Outrageous behavior? Would you say that the professor's conduct is sexual in nature?"

"Very much so," said Jollie, lowering his eyes. "It shames me to say it."

Mr. Bottomly frowned. "Aha—I believe I know the very student you mean. I have been observing her for some time now. She has red hair and an inappropriately prominent bust line, no?"

"Indeed—the very same."

"Indeed, Professor Lebowitz's conduct is certainly outrageous. We at Millard Fillmore do not tolerate that sort of rakish behavior on the part of our employees or teachers, and most especially not our professors! Thank you for coming in and for confirming what I have long thought and suspected. I will speak to Professor Roy. This cannot be allowed to go on—not in this institution, it cannot."

Jollie gave a slow nod. "No, indeed. Proprieties must be observed."

"Can you tell, I mean advise me, I mean, it is necessary that I know the name of the unfortunate recipient of Professor Lebowitz's attentions." Mr. Bottomly leaned forward.

"Her name is Peppy Zipline."

"Ah! The very same! I know her well, I mean *of* her well."

Jollie went on. "She is part of the writing group to which I belong. Jud Roy doubtless is trying to take advantage of her by including the lady in the special project involving the creative writing class. Although I count myself as one of her many admirers, and I suspect that she has feelings for me as well, her writing talent is minimal. It is certain that the professor's interest in her has only to do with his nefarious intentions."

"You wouldn't happen to have her phone number or address, or maybe an e-mail? It will probably be necessary for me to speak with her without Professor Lebowitz knowing of the young lady's and mine correspondence, I mean, of our talking, and it should be alone—privacy, you understand, is a rigorous rule here, and violation thereof is not to be tolerated!"

Jollie was confused for a moment and then realized that Mr. Bottomly was an idiot. "Sir, you are right to take precautions. The man has a nasty temper. He's threatened me with bodily harm several times. The very idea makes me laugh. I study the Eastern philosophy of Jujitsu. I also won several awards for football. Plus, I was quite a wrestler in my high-school days. Ha! I'd like to see that sissy boy try to best me!" Jollie clenched his fists and leaned forward. The two men's faces were less than a foot apart.

"I do not blame you. Disrespecting ladies is an outrageous flaw and a man must step forward to stop, er, curtail the act, whatever and whenever it presents itself. Why, when I was in the navy, we made it our business to protect women, even if they did not ask for it. Why, there we were, doing what men do best. Again, do you have the woman's address and phone number so that I can interview her personally? I will need it right away, sir—I am, after all, the superintendent and a very busy man."

"The young woman does not share her address or phone number with impunity, although I suspect that Jud Roy has used his position to pressure her into giving him her personal information. But she has never shared her address or phone number with me—in fact, she's never shared anything with me, although she'll come around—women always do."

"Ha ha! Well said."

Jollie smiled. "I believe Peppy lives near the Allmart, where I work. She stops by my workplace to chat quite often. She has a flirtatious nature. I, as I said, prefer to wait until conquest is sure. No doubt, my disinterest drove her to Professor Jud Roy Lebowitz. For a short time, anyways—yes, I am sure it will be a very short time."

"A loose woman, so you say? She is easy, then. You mean a woman without standards, an indecent, shameless sort?"

"Indeed, sir, I am both sorry and glad to say so."

"Ha! You are quite the comedian. Thank you, Mr. Inch, for coming in to report this—Peppy Zipline, you say? I will look into the school records and find out more about her with regard to this very serious situation."

Jollie did not want Peppy to look wholly bad. "Mr. Bottomly, allow me to say that in her defense, I believe that Peppy's behavior stems from a need for true love. A need I am prepared to fill in full measure."

"Full measure, you say? Ha ha! Yes, you are certainly quite the cutup Mr. Inch."

After Jollie left, he could still hear the supervisor chuckling behind the office door.

"So strange for a school supervisor. But I suppose a man is what he is," Jollie told a snowman he'd built from some cloud. "Not so much women. Women are never what they seem." He thought of Peppy and sighed.

Unfortunately, Mr. Bottomly did not have time to go through Peppy's records that day. He had an important meeting with the school board that evening.

When Mr. Bottomly presented the idea of increasing attendance at PTA meetings by putting on a play, the school board was enthusiastic until Mr. Bottomly told them that he had arranged for four adult students and their teacher to act in it. Several board members objected to using adults to provide entertainment for the PTA.

Ms. Wing was especially adamant. "The name of the organization is the Parent-Teacher Association, not the Teacher's Parents Association," she said. Her remark drew only a few twitters. School board members are not known for their sense of humor.

Ms. Wing was a forceful and respected member of the board. Everyone knew that Mr. Bottomly was right when he insisted that parents and teachers did not want to see children perform, but no one had ever won an argument with Ms. Wing, so they compromised. The members decided that Ms. Penny's third grade chorus would sing one song at the start of the meeting, and Professor Lebowitz and his four very talented students would end the meeting with their play. Since the meeting took place on Saint Patrick's Day, they decided to have the children sing "Londonderry Air," more commonly known as "O Danny Boy."

At the following class, Jud Roy told the other four Three Musketeers to be at the meeting on time. They sensed his excitement and arrived promptly. "Everyone, everyone, gather around," called Jud Roy, and he waved his arms about the room. "I have an important announcement to make—" Jollie was babbling something about his autobiography being re-released and would not be quiet. Jud Roy raised his voice. "I said, shut up, everyone! We are to put on a play for a live audience!"

Even Jollie shut up. Jud Roy puffed out his chest and announced, "Members of the Three Musketeers, your hour has come. Superintendent Bob Bottomly, also known as the Bouncing-Eye Guy, Squint-Eye, and Eye-Eye, Sailor, has selected our group to write, direct, and perform a play in front of a live—I repeat—a live audience. We will perform our play for an exclusive, very important PTA meeting attended by as many as *one hundred people*. The meeting is on March 17, only one month away. It is imperative that we work together to make the play a success."

Jollie stood up, walked majestically to the front of the room, and stood in front of the professor. He gave a slight bow and said, "Ladies and gentlemen, and especially Peppy, this golden opportunity may never come again. I will lead, and you will follow. I will write and direct the play, and I will be the star. I have been acting since I was a child. In fact, I was the leading man in a well-known soap opera, the name of which escapes me."

Jud Roy stepped out from behind Jollie. "Jollie, sit down or you're out of the play!" he ordered. Jollie sauntered over to his chair.

There will be no 'star,'" Jud Roy cautioned. Remember, everyone, we must all work together. This play is very important. I am the teacher, so I will make all decisions, and all of you have to do exactly what I tell you to without argument or dumb questions. I will play a key role, and I will write and direct the play—however, I will allow that some of you may make suggestions, if time allows."

Jollie argued. "You have the proper serious attitude as to the importance of this venture, but are a blithering ass when it comes to artistic endeavorment. We need someone with experience to write and direct the play. My being here is our good fortune. I allow you may take a key role, but I must be the lead and write and direct the play."

"Ridiculous," said Jud Roy. "I will allow you the lead, but I am the teacher, so I will be the director. And you're the ass. *Endeavorment* isn't a word, any more than Scandinavia is a country."

"What? I'm confused," Peppy said.

Jollie ignored her. "Oh, really? You dare tell me what a word is? I suppose it was ridiculous when I sold you out to Bottomly, fool!"

He's the jerk who wrote the letters complaining about me to Bottomly, thought Jud Roy. "You rat!" he yelled.

"Snake!" hollered Jollie.

"Weasel!"

"Pig!"

Jud Roy ran out of animals to call Jollie. "Dammit, I'm the teacher, I select myself as the director, and there's nothing you can do about it."

Jollie knew that, as a student, he could not possibly control the entire project, but he also knew that he could control a large part of it if he became a huge enough pain in the ass. He would take what he could get.

Jollie calmed down. "Let's talk about this. I'm sure we can find a way to best serve the interests of all. Although I think it is a mistake, you can write and direct, and I will play the lead and be on stage the most."

Jud Roy knew that the more Jollie was on stage, the more likely the play would fail, and he refused to negotiate on that point. Pointing a finger at Jollie, the professor warned, "Anyone wants to argue with me, they're off the play and I replace them with the bald man who writes haikus."

"Shut up, Jollie, shut up," hissed Leslie, Dino, and Peppy.

Once again, Peppy took great pleasure watching the two men argue—later, she would rethink it while she lay in bed and hugged her stuffed bunny. Dino was too unfocused to realize there was a problem at all. Leslie, being the brightest of the five, would have been the best choice for a leader, but none of the group would have followed. The men's argument took a brief hiatus and then started up again, until everyone in the group got pissed off and, one by one, they stomped out. Leslie was the last to go. All five of The Three Musketeers spent the weekend absorbing the terrifying reality of going on stage.

At Monday's meeting, even Jollie was ready to listen to Jud Roy.

"Now let's get started," the professor said. "We will begin at the beginning—the first act. It must grab the audience, make them sit up and take notice."

Peppy was eager to speak. "OK, that sounds good. Now, let's talk about what we're going to wear. I was thinking my short pink dress or the tight red one. With my black push-up bra? Or maybe something classier. I have a darling sparkly formal gown that I've never worn. Or my spring suit—although it's the wrong season for yellow. My green sweater looks good, it fits perfectly, and I have a gold locket that everyone comments on. It was a present from an ex-boyfriend, and I'm pretty sure it's real gold too. Also, I have my waitress uniform. If I roll the skirt up, it—"

Jollie interrupted. "I'm going to go for a pinstripe blue suit with my Hermes tie. Just to be quirky, I'll wear bright orange running shoes. In fact, why don't we do a play about a sports figure? Maybe Joe Tameless? Instead of a button-down shirt, I'll wear a jersey with a big black *JT* on the front."

Jud Roy retorted, "Why? Because Joe Tameless would sue our asses off, that's why. I will play a doctor and wear a fresh, crisp lab coat and a stethoscope—and black pants, doctors always wear black pants. I'll have lots and lots of pens clipped in the pockets of my lab coat."

"Where the hell are you going to get a stethoscope? At Toys and Us?" Jollie smirked.

"Good idea!" said Jud Roy.

"Since Joe Tameless is so easily offended, perhaps you could some made-up sports figure," Peppy suggested.

Dino interrupted. "I will wear my favorite outfit, my multicolored silk caftan that opens in front. Underneath my caftan, I'll wear a festooned belly dancer's costume I made myself. When I walk on and off the stage, the caftan will sweep aside and treat the audience to a glimpse of my nether regions."

"Shouldn't we decide what the story is before we talk about what to wear?" asked Leslie sensibly.

"Maybe…and then again, maybe not," said Jud Roy. "I was hired to teach Creative Writing because I am creative. A story might interfere with the creative process. One thing for sure, we will end the play with a death! That's how all the best stories end, so that's what we'll do."

Everyone loved the idea of a death, especially Jollie.

"Yes," he said. "A slow, lingering death that will tear at peoples' hearts. The dying person will of course be the lead. That would be me."

Jud Roy pictured Jollie dying and agreed that he should play the lead.

Before they all left, Jud Roy called out to them, "Think about death! Remember our play will end with a death!"

At the next meeting, the group discussed the components of a good play.

Leslie was adamant about proper formatting and structure. For once, she was the first to speak. "We must work together, as four fingers and a thumb, the thumb being our instructor, Professor Lebowitz."

"I should be the thumb," Jollie interrupted.

Leslie had strong opinions about the thumb. "You should certainly not be the thumb—you're more like a middle finger. What I'm trying to say is that the play must be well written and well organized."

Jud Roy spoke next. "Wrong, wrong, wrong. Organization doesn't matter; it's all about excessive drama—any director knows that. Who's that Italian guy? Linguine? Listen, art, whether it's music, plays, or finger painting, is like a drug—nobody cares whether or not it makes sense, so long as it makes entertainment."

Dino agreed. "Jud Roy Lebowitz, you are correct. Histrionics are always entertaining. Our play should open like the soft touch of an invisible hand, that guides, then changes to a clenched, bloody fist knocking on the door of hell. The best way to judge art is by how much it upsets people."

Jollie thought the process should be simpler. "Drama? History? Screw that—every story needs a hero. Somebody to do something heroic, like save the world from an enemy. Then the enemy tries to kill him in some devious, cruel manner. The hero escapes and accidently drops the bad guy from a helicopter. The bad guy dies and makes a messy splat right in the middle of town. Hundreds of people witness it in silence. Then comes the music and credits. I am the obvious choice to play the hero."

Jud Roy agreed. "That hero stuff never fails. At our last meeting, we briefly discussed doing a play about a sports figure—those are mostly about real people, so it hasn't been overused. But first let's focus on coming up with a title. A title that will peak the audience's curiosity and hook them so that they cannot escape the story without knowing the outcome."

"Exactly!" Jollie agreed. "In fact, I was thinking about a title all night long. Shut up, everyone. I've got one no one could possibly resist—listen to this—*Blood, Guts, and Body Secretions*. It's angry and violent but simple and effective. Violence has been a sellout throughout the ages. We could even include some slap-around slapstick like in Laurel and Hardy."

Jud Roy objected. "I might consider some slap-around slapstick, so long as I get to play Hardy, the guy that does all the slapping. However, a little humor goes a long way, and Laurel and Hardy routines have been tedious for years. Besides, we've already discussed why we can't do Joe Tameless, and neither should we risk offending Laurel and Hardy. However, quarterbacks *are* very highly thought of."

No one said anything, so Jud Roy went on.

"OK, since there are no objections, let's go with a quarterback. Now, let's get some suggestions as to the title. We've already agreed that death is the most favorable outcome of the play, so the title should include the word *death*. Suggestions?"

"*Don't Worry, Be Dead?*" suggested Dino.

"Too sing-songy," said Jud Roy.

"*Everyone Cares When a Hero Dies?*" offered Jollie.

"Gives the story away," said Jud Roy.

"Wait a minute! How about *Death of a Quarterback?*" Leslie cried.

Jud Roy thought a moment. "It's perfect! Leslie, you've done it! You got something right. Maybe there's hope for you yet."

"Get real, Jud Roy." Jollie winked at Peppy.

"Piss off." Leslie hissed.

"You know, Jollie, sometimes people say things just to be nice," said Jud Roy. "Leslie has finally made a good suggestion, and I thought I should acknowledge her with a compliment."

Dino stood up and raised her hands. Her armpits were unshaven, and everyone looked away.

"Jud Roy Lebowitz, Jollie Inch, Peppy Zipline, and Leslie Tomatiny—let us be calm. Let us rest a moment and review what we have achieved. Violence, death, and quarterbacks are a good start, but we neglect what we seek to find. We must embrace mystery…for our audience and for ourselves. That way, if we ever need to explain what the play is about, we can always say, 'It's a mystery.' Remember—anything that frightens is sure to fascinate. No zombies though. That's yesterday's news. I speak from experience," she said with authority, and sat down.

"Don't forget sex. A good story has to have sex. Nothing gets an audience's attention like it. Sex is a thing we are all still young enough to agree on," Peppy reminded them.

Jud Roy jumped in. "I like it, Musketeers, I like it. We're actually getting somewhere. Now let's talk about characters. When we know who our characters are, the story will be easy. Since I am a professor, and since I already bought a stethoscope for ten bucks at the Toys and Us, I will be a doctor. I come from a long family of doctors, so it will be an easy part for me to play. Let's see—Leslie is an unattractive person who tends to say dull things, so she will play an obsessed, potato-faced woman who goes insane. We have to have someone to represent the coming of the death—someone earthy—Dino, you'll be death. You can also be the narrator. They're both very short parts, short enough to stop people from wondering why such a homely woman is onstage at all. OK, that takes care of mystery. Peppy is the obvious choice for the sexy broad, and Jollie is the idiot quarterback whose brain has been beaten to mush by countless head slams. At the end of the play, the quarterback will die. Excellent work, everyone, excellent. We have structure, drama, mystery, sex, heroics, professional medical care, and a death—they're gonna love it." Jud Roy was feeling better. "This play, students, may be just the thing—"

"The play's the thing," piped Leslie.

"Very good, Leslie. A play is a thing, as opposed to a person or place, meaning it is a noun. I can see you've been doing your homework," said Jud Roy.

Leslie leveled her eyes. "That 'thing' was Shakespeare." *Idiot-head*, she thought.

"Let's not get ahead of ourselves, Leslie. I think most people know that Shakespeare was not a thing," Jud Roy admonished.

The Three Musketeers spent the rest of the meeting making suggestions and arguing, but things were finally coming together. By the fourth meeting, they were ready to write the play.

Jud Roy began. "Dino will both begin and end the play. She will wear the classic grim-reaper regalia in the final moments after Jollie's demise, when she takes him straight to hell. I guess she can wear the grim-reaper stuff to narrate too."

Dino said, "My multicolored silk caftan looks much nicer and is a far better choice to narrate in. The swirls and colors of this worldly garment will heighten the mystery of the play. Its strange patterns mimic life's ramble into what ordinary people call 'the unknown' and what extraordinary people call 'the known regardless of evidence to the contrary.' I assure you, it will have quite an effect."

"Dammit, Dino—no one wants to see a woman in a caftan!" said Jollie.

"When a woman wears a caftan, it generally means she's got something to hide," said Leslie. "For example, shoplifters wear caftans to steal large items such as prime rib or a leg of lamb." She thought of Larger Billie. He'd had a real talent for identifying shoplifters.

Peppy was wise in the way of fashion. "Really, Dino, a grim-reaper robe and hood are perfect for you. With its volume and length, the robe will hang in graceful sweeps that show your substantial curves to their greatest advantage. Also, a classic grim-reaper's robe is a dark solid color, which is slimming, and your cane will make a lovely accessory when used as a staff."

"Dammit, everyone!" said Jud Roy. "I am your teacher, your director, and your doctor—and I say that Dino will dress as the grim reaper. There's not enough time in the play for her to change from her narrator clothes to her grim-reaper attire, and vice versa, so she'll have to wear the grim-reaper costume throughout the entire play. Now can we all shut up about clothes and get on with it? OK—the first person on stage is obviously the narrator. The narrator needs to prepare the audience as to the horrific nature of our play. Dino, I want you to begin by announcing the name of the play in no uncertain terms."

"Uncertain terms? Do you mean derisively?" Jollie asked.

"Decisively," said Leslie.

"Enough with the adverbs, already!" said Jud Roy. "This is important! In no uncertain terms is what I said, and in no uncertain terms is what I mean. Be bold, be loud, startle them, startle yourself. Remember, the title is *Death of a Quarterback*. As Leslie said, it's just the thing. It has all five of the elements we discussed: sex, death, mystery, a hero, structure, um, well, it has four of the elements, but we don't want to give everything away."

Jud Roy was excited now.

CHAPTER 21

Marketing

● ● ●

JOLLIE'S POSITION AS ALLMART GREETER gave him access to thousands of people whom he could tell about the play, giving special emphasis to his starring role as quarterback. It took Office Smart only a day to print up two hundred pamphlets and a cardboard sign that read:

Death of a Quarterback!
A Football Hero, a Murdering
Doctor, Women, Infidelity, and Death
Don't miss this dramatically thrilling experience spon-
sored by Allmart and starring the incompatible
Jollie Inch
What Critics Are Saying
WOW!—*The San Francisco Good Times*
OH, BOY!—*The Snooze News*
YEE-HAW!—*None of Your Business Journal*
One night only—No Cover Charge
Millard Fillmore Elementary-Adult Education,
1234 Happy Road Ave., Oakland, California
March 17th, 6:00 p.m. to 8:00 p.m. Full
House Theatre, left side of gym

That Saturday, Jollie came in to work a full half hour early. He waited at his usual place, just inside the main doors, for Allmart to open. Around his neck, hung the sign advertising *Death of a Quarterback*. The pamphlets were stuffed in the pockets of his Allmart smock. He held a plastic Bunny-Luv microphone he had borrowed from the toy department.

The weekend crowds were already surging outside the glass doors. At 8:59 a.m., the manager rushed passed Jollie, unlocked the doors, and sped away before anyone could ask him where something was.

Jollie shouted into the microphone. "Attention Allmart shoppers! Today only! Free ice cream!"

The people fell back in stunned silence.

"Welcome—welcome to Allmart. My name is Jollie Inch, star of the much-anticipated theatrical extravaganza, *Death of a Quarterback*. Allmart is hosting a live performance of this critically acclaimed show, also known as a "play". This "play" will raise money for an undisclosed charity event that you would all greatly approve of. Since it is for charity, there is no cover charge. *Death of a Quarterback* may not be appropriate for young children, however, women may come, especially unparticular ladies with liberal values. If you will just form a line, I will pass out the handouts. Please show them to your friends. The handouts may be exchanged for unlimited free ice cream. That's right, I said *free unlimited ice cream*! One handout per customer, please."

The crowd rushed Jollie and fought for the pamphlets. With carts bashing, the storm of enthusiastic shoppers hurried to the ice-cream section and, heedless of brand or flavor, began recklessly filling their carts. The chocolate, the praline, and the strawberry went first, and then the mint chip, the coffee, and all the rest. They even took the rum raisin. It took only ten minutes for the people to deplete the Allmart's entire stock of ice cream. Customers gathered at the cash registers, waving flyers, demanding ice cream, and refusing to pay. Jollie was delighted that his plan had met with such success. He wished he had more flyers.

Mr. Pimpernel wrestled through the crowd of people to where Jollie was maniacally shouting welcomes. When he got to the front door, he fired Jollie on the spot. Jollie thought it most unfair. Mr. Pimpernel had not even given him a chance to explain that it was all a brilliant publicity stunt, and most remarkably pulled off. Why, for less than the cost of a newspaper ad, Allmart had welcomed the morning's customers with free ice cream, which is the best kind of welcome of all.

Damn! Jollie thought. He had never shown Peppy the No Access to the Public area.

Mr. Pimpernel sent the head office a video of the incident, with an explanation of what had happened. The head office sent the video to Allmart's legal department. Allmart's legal department advised the head office that they should have all Allmart employees review the video and sign a form stating that they understood that giving away free stuff was unacceptable. In addition, the head office and the legal department discontinued the position of Allmart Greeter for all Allmarts, including those overseas.

However, the media loved the video and the idea of free ice cream. In fact, every single Allmart store in the world would take in more money the year of the ice-cream incident than in any other year in the history of Allmart.

CHAPTER 22

Men Behaving Badly

● ● ●

JOLLIE FILED FOR UNEMPLOYMENT AND settled in for long days of much-missed daytime television. He had plenty of time now to do some serious research on the Internet. His first entry was *Professor Jud Roy Lebowitz*. The only thing he found was an image of Jud Roy's ad. Someone had written "Illiterate Nincompoop" over Jud Roy's name. Jollie printed out the ad and went to see Mr. Bottomly.

The knock on the door startled the superintendent. He hadn't received so many visitors since—well, he couldn't remember exactly, not that it mattered or should be of concern, but, um, he was particularly, well, most surprised and very amazed. Reluctantly, he turned off the TV. He had been watching his favorite Hitler documentary. It vexed him when people arrived unannounced.

When he opened the door, there stood Jollie.

Mr. Bottomly stepped aside to allow Jollie to enter. "Come in, Mr. Inch. No appointment again, I see. What can I do for you? Is it about that wanton woman again?" he asked hopefully. He spoke in a flat voice he imagined disguised his base interest in Peppy.

Jollie tried to match Mr. Bottomly's deep voice. "This is a much more serious matter, sir. Again, it involves Mr. Lebowitz. I believe he has lied about his credentials and gotten his job under false pretenses, which constitutes a criminal offense. The printout of this flyer gave rise to my suspicions." Jollie slid Jud Roy's ad across the superintendent's desk. "I draw your attention to the words *Illiterate Nincompoop* written across the name.

I checked the Amazon website. He has never written a book. When I Googled him, I found no evidence that he is a professor. In fact, I found nothing at all."

If Jollie's accusations were true, Mr. Bottomly would have to let Jud Roy go. At first, the superintendent silently rejoiced, and then realized that dismissing Jud Roy would mean canceling the current semester's creative writing class, and Peppy might stop coming to school. Moreover, they'd have a hell of a time finding a suitable teacher to replace Jud Roy.

Mr. Bottomly threw up his hands in mock horror. "I cannot believe it. An instructor at Millard Fillmore? Are you sure? Are you positive? Jud Roy Lebowitz told me himself that he graduated from the prestigious university *Les Belles de Escribir* in Paris, France. Although France's cowardice embarrassed all of Europe in World War 2, Paris has some of the finest learning institutions in the world. Professor Roy must have written something, maybe when he was in France. So long, I mean, as long as it was read somewhere by someone who didn't know him, even if that someone did it as a favor, he is a writer, is he not? As to the title 'professor,' that is open to interpretation, or opinion might be the better word. In my opinion, that he is here teaching at Millard Fillmore qualifies him as a professor." Mr. Bottomly's wandering eye bounced about.

There was a knock on the door. Both men jumped. "Come in!" the supervisor called out. Jud Roy did so. When he saw Jollie, he gritted his teeth.

"I suspected as much. You dare spread tales about me? You, a has-been ex-Allmart greeter, do you dare?" Jud Roy was actually shouting.

"Professor Lebowitz! Control yourself! That's no way for an American to act!" ordered Mr. Bottomly. Jud Roy did not even look at him.

"How's the writing business, Professor?" Jollie shouted.

"Not quite as good as the business I give Peppy!" screamed Jud Roy.

Mr. Bottomly stood up and brandished a sandwich he'd been eating earlier. "What! What is this I'm hearing? Your comments about this fair lady are completely inappropriate."

"You know, Clown face, you think you got Peppy because you're something special. Well, I happen to know that Peppy thinks *everyone* is something special—she sure chased after me!" Jollie said.

Mr. Bottomly threw his sandwich toward the trashcan and missed. "Men! Men! Stop this minute. This is a school, not a sporting event! Get ahold of yourselves, or I will cancel the play, altogether, and in no undue haste, I assure you, you can bet on that!"

Jud Roy ran his hand through his curly hair, and Jollie fiddled with his Hermes tie. Jollie calmed his voice and said evenly, "You should know, Superintendent Bottomly, that Jud Roy has a history of lying. He not only lied about his credentials, but he lied to my supervisor at Allmart and got me fired. The Allmart proprietor, Mr. Pimpernel, was very apologetic about having to let me go—in fact, he wrote letters to Allmart executives throughout the country, pleading that I remain with the firm. At the time of my termination, Mr. Pimpernel was considering me for a substantial promotion. Sadly, company policy dictates that Allmart terminate an employee if even a single member of the purchasing public lodges a racist complaint. Jud Roy falsely accused me of remarking on his Jewish heritage, which I suspect he tries to hide." He turned toward Jud Roy.

Jud Roy threw out his chest and took a step toward Jollie. "Oh, really? Well, let me tell you something, no Jew ever got hung for stealing horses!"

"Gentlemen! Gentlemen! We were discussing Ms. Zipline!" said Mr. Bottomly.

Jud Roy and Jollie stopped shouting and turned toward Mr. Bottomly. Peppy's file lay on his desk. Her student photo smiled up at the three men.

"Peppy been around?" asked Jud Roy sarcastically.

Mr. Bottomly took several deep breaths.

"Now, Gentlemen—it is clear that we all care about this unfortunate young lady." His good eye looked to the ceiling a moment. "Indeed... indeed, it is that very capacity to care that sets us apart from the animal kingdom and its ever-present stupidity."

Mr. Bottomly pressed his hands together. "Let us be wise, then...let us be men. Consider for a moment how our thoughtless actions could irreversibly damage Millard Fillmore Elementary-Adult Education. Consider how its high standards and liberal policies benefit us all, especially the migrant laborers who attend our English classes and the old people who come to learn basic computer skills. We have responsibilities—my responsibility as a superintendent, Professor Lebowitz's responsibility as an instructor, and Mr. Inch's responsibility as the star of our school play, a play, I might add, which has been sanctioned by the PTA. I am ordering an end to this matter this day! Professor Lebowitz, Mr. Itch—leave this woman alone! Now, extract yourselves from my office, both of you, with no uncertain haste! No, I will not shake your hand." His eye jumped.

As soon as they were gone, Mr. Bottomly picked up Peppy's file. He liked looking at the picture, liked reading the file's contents, and admiring the curly way she signed her name. Her e-mail tantalized him—Peppyzip@email.com. Yes—he would write her an official e-mail. Mr. Bottomly wrote, asking her to meet with him in his office. She answered almost immediately, suggesting they meet the following morning at ten.

The next morning, Mr. Bottomly wore his best sports coat and tie. His hair glistened with hair oil, and he'd spent twenty dollars having his nails buffed and manicured. His neck and face smelled of aftershave from a bottle that was so old the label had faded into nothingness. In a fit of ingenuity, he had covered his bad eye with a patch. Mr. Bottomly looked into a tiny compact mirror and decided that the patch was rather dashing.

"Never saw him without that pirate patch again," remarked Jollie from his cloud.

Mr. Bottomly sat, hands on the desk, gazing into the still quiet. The television was off. When the knock came, his heart caught in his throat. He checked his watch. It was precisely ten o'clock. She was exactly on time.

"Come in," he said in a crooked voice. The door opened. The silhouette of Peppy's lovely form filled the doorway.

"Come in, dear lady. You must be Ms. Zipline. Thank you for responding so promptly to my e-mail," said Mr. Bottomly. "Coffee? Or maybe a Diet Coke?" He held up a porcelain coffee cup and a crystal glass.

"No, nothing, thank you." Peppy sat down. "I sure was surprised when you asked me to meet with you. I'm eager to find out why."

"Glad to know you're eager," said Mr. Bottomly. "It is a grave, a most serious matter, I'm afraid. A great wrong has been done. Yes, it pains me to, so sorry to say, but it involves a man's disorderly conduct. Do you know of whom I am talking about?"

"Why, yes, I think so. Is it about my sleeping with Professor Jud Roy Lebowitz?"

"My concern, my worry and concern, is this—Ms. Zipline, my worry is that Professor Lebowitz may have used his position to take advantage of you. Did he? Take advantage of you, I mean? I will need details."

Peppy sighed. "Why don't we just get this over with, Fisheye? I know what you want, you know that I know, and two knows is a no-no."

"Ha!" Jollie laughed from the cloud.

Mr. Bottomly was hurt by Peppy's remark. *Fisheye—so she noticed before,* he thought. But he was no quitter when it came to romancing a good-looking woman of dubious reputation.

"I understand your feelings. A beautiful lady like yourself must often deal with sloppy, undisciplined men, men who do not deserve to be called men, as such—undeserving men who should not be called at all, no, not at all, neither on the phone nor in the street in front of public opinion. If you don't mind a compliment, your red hair is lovely."

"You—really like it?"

"It is like a fire exploding from your head. Did you know, Ms. Zipline— that sounds so formal, doesn't it? May I call you Peppy? Such a charming name."

"Yes. May I call you Bob?"

"I would rather you called me Superintendent," Mr. Bottomly replied.

"Uh—OK, Mr. Superintendent," Peppy said. *Professor Lebowitz and Superintendent—men and their titles!*

Mr. Bottomly lowered his voice. "Do not be disturbed by my adhering to rules and regulations. It is my military training that guides me. As an ex-navy man, I am accustomed to rules and the importance of doing, er, being so. That being said, I sometimes forget that women have softer characters—therefore, I permit you to cry a little should my rough ways startled you, so long as you have the goodness to do it quietly."

"Mr. Superintendent, I'm not going to cry," said Peppy.

Mr. Bottomly continued. "As I was saying, such a charming name. We seem to have a lot, I mean to say, a great many things in common. I, a gentleman—you, a lady. A man and a woman, created for a single purpose, a purpose for which God intended and gave to this great country. Yes... how true that is. Ah-hem! But, let me tell you about myself. I have been superintendent of Millard Fillmore Elementary-Adult Education for fifteen years. For the performance of my superintenderary duties, I am justifiably paid a salary commiserate with my responsibilities. You have probably wondered how this school came to be named for Millard Fillmore, one of the greatest presidents our country has ever known."

"President of what?" asked Peppy.

"Your little joke amuses. It makes me laugh most heartily. Ha ha! I do so love to have a good time, and I see that I could have one with you. May I, Peppy? Could you show me a good time?"

"Well, you make me laugh too, Mr. Superintendent," Peppy said lamely.

"I am quite the comic, yes. How I often evoked laughter for the men on the USS *Stricthand*—I had 'em rolling in the aisles—if it had been the army, they would have been rolling in the trenches. Ha ha!" laughed Mr. Bottomly. He cleared his throat and sneezed.

"Who was the guy the school was named after again?" asked Peppy.

"Pardon me—we were speaking of how the school was named Millard Fillmore. I named the school, yes, me—I named this establishment. The city council of the Oakland came to me, and I named the school for my distant relative on my mother's side. I think, I mean, I believe he was my eleven times great-grandfather, which accounts for the distance you see."

Peppy frowned at the wall.

"My great-grandfather times eleven left a considerable fortune, which I eventually inherited, little diminished, that is to say, and I received a huge lot of the money, in fact the family's entire estate, to include the holdings of the well-heeled socialites in Paris." Mr. Bottomly leaned back in his chair.

"Paris? How I love to travel," said Peppy. "In fact, I am very well-traveled. I went once to Scandinavia."

"Woo-wee, I have been to Pareee," said Mr. Bottomly, and chortled a bit. "I too have traveled extensively, most often in the service of my country, but throughout the world, always first class, always the highest quality, and in prime luxury, I might add. Oh, yes—I have been to Paris, where Germans marched; I have been to Rome, where all roads lead; I have been to England, where the sun never goes up or down; and I have been to Russia, where no one can remember all the countries because they keep changing their names and nobody gives a damn."

"Have you been to Scandinavia like I have?" asked Peppy. "It's pretty far away too."

"Of course—a lovely country, Scandinavia. Let me give you my private phone number in case Professor Lebowitz should bother you again. We could discuss any future problems over an expensive dinner at the Dead Lobster."

"Superintendent Bottomly, I have to go to work," Peppy said.

"Will you be in class this evening?" asked Mr. Bottomly.

"Yes."

"I knew you were a consciences student. *Ow-doo-ware, then, mon petit.* That means, 'Do I wait to see you, little petted one?' And I do."

"Good-bye, Superintendent Bottomly." With a shake of her bottom, Peppy left. Something about Mr. Bottomly unnerved her. She needed to think seriously about his offer. He was offering a lot, and she really was getting tired of bowling, Allmart, and Jud Roy Lebowitz.

The superintendent decided to overlook Jollie's accusations about Professor Lebowitz. Mr. Bottomly had already lectured the professor about student complaints, and it didn't seem fair to say anything more after he'd given the professor an opportunity to prove himself by performing for the PTA. Besides, the school board had already sent a letter to the parents about the meeting and the play, so Jud Roy Lebowitz had to stay on.

CHAPTER 23

Men Behaving Very Badly

● ● ●

Jud Roy semi dozed in a hot bath. His head hurt. It was only yesterday that he, Jollie, and Superintendent Bottomly had met, but it seemed a long, long time ago, and Jud Roy had heard nothing. That was good—but maybe it was bad. If only Jollie would just disappear. But even if such a miracle happened, the play was only two weeks away. He'd have to work with Jollie—and Peppy too. *What was wrong with Peppy lately?* Jud Roy frowned and a stinging pain raced across his head. Peppy had hardly spoken to him for a week. She was probably concerned about how to dress for the play. Poor Peppy. Everyone would be looking at her. He could marry that woman. She was that hot. Plus, marrying Peppy would burn both Jollie and Bottomly. If it didn't work out, one of his Lebowitz relatives could do the divorce for free.

When the phone rang, Peppy was trying on clothes. She had finally decided to wear her sparkly red gown with the slit up the side. She'd worn it only once, to her cousin's wedding, and was glad for the opportunity to show it off again. Definitely, the red dress. It was perfect. She picked up the quacking phone. Peppy liked animal ring tones.

"Hi, Jud Roy," she said impatiently. She still had to select the jewelry to go with the dress.

"Hey, baby. We on for Burgers and Booze on Saturday?" Jud Roy sighed, thinking about last Saturday and the wonders of Peppy.

"As usual, six o'clock," said Peppy. She wanted to say, "No, let's just be friends." Peppy was tired of Jud Roy, but she didn't want to dump him while they were working together on the play. She'd have to sleep with him awhile longer, but that was no big deal because he was quick. Saturday at six o'clock. She looked at her calendar and sighed.

Jollie paced back and forth in his apartment. He knew that Jud Roy and Peppy met Saturday nights at Burgers and Booze, and this time, he would be there too. He'd start out casual-like, say he just happened to come by. He would look surprised to see them, and then say he had something important to speak about with the professor. The men would excuse themselves and step outside a moment. Then, Jollie would tell Jud Roy that he had seen Peppy going into Bottomly's office the day after the two of them had been there. He would remind Jud Roy that Bottomly had the legal right to fire a teacher for having carnal relations with his students. If Peppy had gone to complain about the professor's conduct, then for his own good, Jud Roy had to give her up.

Jud Roy, Peppy, and Jollie waited anxiously for Saturday. It finally came.

The professor waited at Burgers and Booze. It was six fifteen, Peppy, as usual, was late, and Jud Roy, as usual, didn't mind because she always showed up looking great. The professor easily spotted her by the swing of her hips. He waved her over and took her arm. When they walked into the restaurant, everyone turned to look at Peppy.

Burgers and Booze always smelled of pickles and grease. It was crowded, and the couple had to block an elderly woman with a cane and shove their way to a table just vacated by three tattooed teenagers. Peppy plopped herself down, being careful to hike her skirt up.

Meanwhile, Jollie sat at a far corner table near the back of the restaurant, sucking on a beer. Looking around, he noticed a young woman's face. *Damn! Is that Leslie by the pool table? Are the three of them on a double date plus one? Ha! Not likely. Wait a minute—I might be able to use Leslie to make Peppy jealous. Who wouldn't choose me over a talentless jerk who dresses like a clown—no taste at all.*

Jollie gripped handfuls of fluff from the cloud. He stroked his Hermes tie.

Leslie was in the very back of the restaurant, studying a pool game and trying to predict the trajectory of the balls. She was too engrossed to notice Jollie, Jud Roy, or Peppy. Jollie elbowed his way to the pool table and sidled up to her. She felt a man pressing against her and turned her head and smiled, and then winced when she saw it was Jollie. He snaked his arm around her.

"Hello, Leslie," he said.

"Hello," she said blankly and tried to concentrate on the pool table. But he would not shut up.

"Delighted to see you, my dear. Always a pleasure." Jollie stifled a burp.

"I didn't know you came here," Leslie snapped. "Next time, I'll go to the Hoegaarden where there are decent men who don't swill beer and burp. Just yesterday, a guy bought me a glass of wine there."

Leslie had indeed been the lucky recipient of a free glass of wine. A bald headed man had spilled hers when his arthritic arm shot out and knocked over her glass. He insisted on replacing her wine, with a name brand, even.

Jollie pretended the burp came from somebody else. "Swilling and burping are such vulgar habits." He glared at a handsome, well-dressed man with perfect hair leaning against the counter. Jollie talked on.

"They know me well at the Hoegaarden. Their wine list is all right, but a bit more limited than I'm used to. I'm a wine drinker too—more of a taster, I should say. I generally stick to the French varietals, although they can be costly and difficult to find. From the time I was eight years old, my mother packed wine in my lunch box so that I could eat my pâté sandwich properly. She was very particular about her pâté. She raised the goose herself, and my father force-fed it hummingbird seed to enlarge the liver. I come from very fine people. My great-great-great-grandfather, a swashbuckling vaquero type, had his story told in a history book—his name was Justin Sam Le Barge."

"Really? I never heard of a—hey, wait a minute!" Leslie remembered. "Wasn't he in that book, *True Grits of the West*? I seem to remember an entire town held a festival to celebrate the hanging of a Justin Le Barge when they found him guilty of several counts of horse thievery. In fact, the tree he was hung from is still there, in what is now Walnut Creek, formally known as The Corners."

"Good area, Walnut Creek."

"Anyways this book claims that most American cowboys were lying, filthy, lice-ridden drifters who stole anything they could get their hands on. Cowboys had few if any children because rigorous horseback riding squashes the scrotum and raises the temperature in the balls, which decreases sperm count."

"Yeah, well that can happen," said Jollie.

"So, your great-great-great-grandfather was a horse thief?"

Jollie tried to look sexy by knitting his bushy, black eyebrows together. He lowered his voice. "Justin Le Barge was no horse thief—the truth was that jealous men hung him because the women loved his bravado and free-wheeling style." He tried unsuccessfully to raise an eyebrow.

All the while he talked, Jollie was glancing over Leslie's shoulder at Peppy and Jud Roy. When Leslie turned to see what he was looking at, Jollie quickly explained away his interest.

"You have probably noticed how my eyes keep going to the middle table. When it is quieter, I stand up there—yes, at such a height—I stand on that very table, the one in the middle, and read my work to the customers, not what I share with the class but my very best stuff, the stuff that intimidates ordinary people. Knowing my work, you probably would not be surprised to hear this, but I was singled out and acknowledged as remarkable when I was only eight years old. At the time, a Professor Big Sky, who is, interestingly enough, related to Pocahontas, the famous Indian princess, insisted I join her class for creatively gifted special people. I was a big favorite there at only eight years old."

Leslie was sick of it. She was speaking up more and more, and it felt good.

"Jollie, nobody believes your bullshit, and you're not going to be some kind of superstar. One day, you'll wake up and discover you lived your entire life without ever having moved."

"Oh, I'll move. I'll move through the ages. But right now, I merely want to enjoy the company of a beautiful woman."

"Peppy's over there with Jud Roy—and I'm not buying you a drink. Didn't I say that a guy bought me a glass of wine at the Hoegaarden?"

"Hey, Leslie!" Peppy had seen the two of them.

Leslie didn't answer, but Jollie did. "Oh, Peppy, darling…I'm over here," he called. Jollie leaned in toward Leslie. "She must have smelled my cologne," he whispered.

"Shhh!" Jud Roy hissed in Peppy's ear. "Let's get out of here before they notice we're here. Jollie and Leslie come here a lot together—I think they're alcoholics."

Instead, Peppy jumped up and began pushing her way toward the pool tables. Jud Roy followed closely behind. Peppy loved to hear people criticize one another. She hissed back at Jud Roy. "I suspected they were drunks. Leslie's always talking bikers and bars. I wish you could hear the way she talks about the men in her life. She thinks she knows so much, and I hear she has a fat boyfriend. And now Jollie—boy, she's really scraping the bottom of the barrel."

Peppy stopped talking. They had reached Jollie and Leslie.

Jud Roy spoke first. "Leslie, Jollie—I had no idea you were a couple."

"We're two people; that's it," Leslie said snottily.

Jud Roy looked surprised. "Leslie, I do not like your tone. Being two people is nothing to be ashamed of—an individual may be ashamed of being stupid or ugly, and even rightly so, and two people may be ashamed of one another, but the shame is really the shame of the shamee. Shame can last an entire lifetime and often does. I gave a lecture some years ago on that very topic. I must say, you both look very well together. You have so much in common."

Leslie frowned. She stood next to Jud Roy, whom she hated, and Peppy stood next to Jollie, whom she couldn't stand, although his obsession with her was a turn on. Jud Roy and Jollie stood across from each other. Both men wanted to leave the restaurant with either Peppy or both women or, better yet, with Peppy and the blonde at the counter.

Jollie began. "Jud Roy—or perhaps I should say Professor Lebowitz—I have something important to say. Peppy Zipline is a beautiful woman."

Peppy smiled and turned around to see if any of the other customers had heard.

Jollie continued. "However, Professor Lebowitz, I am concerned that if you continue to consort with her, you will lose your position. We're only two weeks away from the PTA meeting. To leave when we have almost finished our play, Professor, would be as criminal as your shocking behavior with women. When I think of how hard I've worked! Would you disappoint the members of the entire PTA? Professor, only consider what you are doing! When the theater-going public recognizes *Death of a Quarterback* for what it is, when that inevitable day comes and it opens on a Broadway stage, the world will recognize me for what I am—playwright, actor, thespian. And you—you would not only keep your job, you could say that you knew me, that you worked with Jollie Inch."

Leslie felt sick. "I've gotta go," she said.

"Oh, Leslie—I'm so sorry you can't stay. Well, if you must go, you must go. Hurry along now," said Peppy. Leslie rushed off to her bomb shelter.

"Well, isn't this nice!" Peppy said brightly. She thrust out a hip and smiled.

Jud Roy grabbed her arm, pulled her away from Jollie, and stood in front of her. Peppy sensed trouble, and she skittered behind the counter, which made an almost perfect princess balcony. The other women joined her, and the ladies clutched one another, and trembled and squealed.

The two men squared off and fairly growled. Alert customers sat up and waited to see what would happen. Some placed bets. The odds were on Jud Roy because he was the fatter of the two.

"Get outta this bar, and don't come back!" Jud Roy ordered.

"Make me!" yelled Jollie.

The gloves were off.

Neither Jollie nor Jud Roy had ever been in a fight, and they didn't want to be in a fight now. Whenever two cowardly men threaten one another with bodily injury, the most likely outcome is that one will eventually announce that the other isn't worth the trouble, they exchange a few more insults, and then both of them walk away. The men were now circling one another like simian boxers. After ten minutes of circling, the other patrons stopped watching and returned to their hamburgers.

It was time to wrap it up. "Aw, he's not worth the trouble," Jud Roy hollered loudly.

Everyone waited to hear what Jollie would say back. Jollie faced the counter where Peppy stood, yawning. He was determined to make a good impression and to win this beautiful woman, damn the cost.

It's going to happen. It's really going to happen, thought Jollie. He was terrified but resolute. His eye spied a plastic catsup bottle.

Jollie grabbed the bottle and squirted catsup on Jud Roy, covering the professor's shirt with sticky wet gore. Jud Roy responded by emptying a Greek salad on Jollie's head. Chunks of cheese matted his hair, lettuce leaves papered his skin, and rivulets of oily dressing streamed down his face. A woman screamed. Both men grabbed butter knives and began circling. The knives were plastic, but the danger felt real, and a horrified Jud Roy threw his aside. Jollie swished his knife back and forth and advanced toward Jud Roy, who ran behind the bar, snatched up the Coke gun, and blasted Jollie full in the face. Blinded, Jollie stumbled and dropped the knife. Jud Roy seized the advantage and ran out from behind the counter toward the ice machine intending to arm himself with chunks of ice. He tripped over Jollie, who had regained his sight and was trying to escape by crawling under a table. The two men grappled, slipped, and slid along the floor into tables and chairs. Other patrons joined in the fun, hurling drinks, hamburgers, malts, and sensible salads. Except for Jud Roy and Jollie, everyone was having a great time. A crowd gathered around the combatants, cheering and shouting enthusiastic advice. IPhones recorded the latest video sensation.

The owner, a burly man used to loutish behavior, elbowed his way through the crowd, pulled down the shades, and turned off the lights. The restaurant plunged into darkness. Men wandered in dizzy confusion. They stumbled over Jollie and Jud Roy and crashed into booths, tables, and one another. To stand still would have been the smart thing to do, but that required thought not action, so instead the men bashed around yelling curses and threats and hurting themselves. It lasted a full ten minutes before everyone got so damn tired they could barely stand. When the activity dipped, the owner opened the door and everyone rushed out into the safety of the streetlights. Once there, most of the embarrassed patrons went off to other bars to nurse their wounds and calm themselves with alcohol.

Peppy and the other women were unscathed due to their hiding place behind the ice-cream counter. Good thing too—being soft and small, they would have gotten the shit knocked out of them in that fierce, blind battle of hairy men. Jud Roy rushed Peppy out to his car. Jollie watched, dejected, and then walked to the Smells Cargo parking lot, where he saw his car had a ticket.

"Almost won that one…almost," said Jollie from the cloud, thinking about what Peppy would have done if he had.

CHAPTER 24

Leslie Gets Even Sadder

● ● ●

JOLLIE PLAYED IN THE CLOUD fluff with his toes. He watched Leslie. She was not pretty, but he liked to watch her.

Leslie got up early the next day feeling particularly lonely. At the bar the night before, she had left alone while all the others stayed on having fun. Nobody wanted her. What she needed was a walk—a long, meandering walk, where no one would see her and guess that she had no place to go.

She had walked almost eight miles when a car pulled up. A window on the passenger side rolled down, and a woman's beautiful face looked out.

"Hey, Leslie! Do you need a ride?" asked Peppy.

She's offering me a ride? Leslie wondered.

Leslie did need a ride. She'd been walking aimlessly for a long, long time, and was hopelessly lost. When she got into the car, she noticed that, rather than her usual immodest attire, Peppy was wearing clothes that were comfortable and conservative.

Peppy was friendly. "I'm on my way home from a modeling job. Did I tell you I model clothes for Sunnyside Retirement Home? The ladies there can't get out, so they put on fashion shows with stretchy clothing designed for pain-free dressing."

"Oh?"

"Yes, and I get a twenty-five dollar gift certificate every time I model, so that makes me a professional. At the end of the show, I give it away to the best-looking old lady. Funny thing is that the old ladies there are looking worse and worse—almost wretched, really. It's getting hard to choose who to give the certificate to, but I always find someone. I'm actually very charitable and kind, although a lot of people don't believe it because I'm so good looking. That's why I picked you up. Plus, a remarkably handsome old man follows me home every time I model, and I needed protection. He uses a walker to get around, but he's still pretty spry."

"Handsome old men aside, you actually look very nice dressed conservatively. I almost respect you," said Leslie.

Both ladies were silent—but Leslie could tell that Peppy wanted to talk.

"Um—Leslie. Leslie, what do you think of Jud Roy? I mean, what do you think of Jud Roy and me?"

Leslie stared at Peppy. "Well, he certainly seems fond of you," she said stupidly. "Peppy, could you not look at yourself in the mirror while you're driving?"

Peppy pretended to dab a tear. "I thought he was crazy about me too—but Leslie, he's changed. About a month ago, he called and said he got Jollie fired from Allmart—he was actually bragging about it, said this big guy punched Jollie and he started to cry. I told him, 'Yeah, great,' and I laughed. Now, I feel almost bad. God knows I can't stand Jollie, but I wouldn't want to see him get beat up—not too badly, anyways. I really am a very kind person, no *really*, I am. I was going to go talk to the manager who fired him—it was probably all Jud Roy's fault. Can you believe what a bastard that guy is? Most men are."

"Wow! I knew Jud Roy hated Jollie, but getting someone beat up and fired?" Leslie was shocked at such uncivility.

"I'll say! And a couple days after that, Superintendent Bottomly calls me in to tell me that Jud Roy's attentions to me are inappropriate. Then Bottomly asks me out to dinner."

"Outrageous!" exclaimed Leslie. "Why don't you tell them both to leave you alone?" She would never have had the courage to do such a thing, but Peppy might.

"Yeah, old Fisheye," Peppy said, ignoring Leslie's remark. "Did you know the school was named for a relative of his? Except for his eye, he's

OK. He told me he has a doctor's degree in something, and I think he makes a lot of money."

Peppy was quiet for a moment.

"You know, it's not always easy being gorgeous. People like me because I'm so stunningly beautiful. Whereas you, if people like you, they like you for yourself. No one would ever think of liking you for your looks."

"Yeah, thanks, Peppy. Lucky me. Well, poor thing, so you've got Jud Roy, Jollie, and now Bottomly after you. Well, well, poor little you. I don't like Jollie either, but what Jud Roy did was terrible. Peppy, please stop looking in the mirror when you're driving."

"Terrible-bad," agreed Peppy. "I've been wondering about that manager who hit Jollie. He must be a pretty big guy—I wonder what he looks like. Maybe we should go back to Allmart and try to get Jollie's job back."

"Yes," said Leslie. "That would be the decent thing to do—decent, like not looking in the mirror when you're driving a friend across town. Peppy? Come on, you look just fine. You always do."

"Really?" Peppy gazed into the mirror again.

Leslie was thoughtful. "I never liked Jollie, but it's sad that he lost his job." She remembered moving to Oakland with no money to escape her mother's house. Whenever he heard Leslie defend him, Jollie cried a little into the cloud. "Oh, why Leslie and not Peppy?"

"You know, Jud Roy would be royally pissed if Jollie got his job back," Peppy said.

Leslie thought of her mother again and bit her nails.

"Leslie!" Peppy said, "Leslie, Jollie's being fired isn't worth ruining your hands!"

"No, no. It's not that. Can I tell you something?"

"Sure. I've shared secrets about Jud Roy. Don't tell anyone what I said about Bottomly, okay? He's, well, he's not so bad. Got that freaky eye, you know. God, I'm tired. Modeling can be tough. So, what's your big secret? I won't tell," said Peppy.

Leslie sniffed. "It's not a secret. It's about my old boyfriend, Larger Billie. Peppy, he's large—really large—and I slept with him, not once, but a bunch of times. But he was good to me, and I can't stop thinking about him. He was really good to me, Peppy. He gave me money so I could move away from Livermore, away from my horrible mother and her disgusting roommates. Larger didn't have a lot of money, he wasn't a professor or a superintendent or anything, but he gave me money to go. Men are not all bastards."

"How interesting," Peppy said politely. "Hey, we should go to Allmart. That's what we should do. Let's go to Allmart and talk to that big hunk of manager."

"Sure, let's go. You know, Peppy, when I first met you, I thought you were some kind of brainless floozy. Now I know that a brainless floozy can also be kind." Leslie wondered if Peppy might turn out to be a friend.

"Thanks, Leslie. I always thought you were dull and stupid. Let's go to Allmart and talk to that manager that beat up Jollie. Then we can shop. We'll pick up some beer and ice cream. Allmart has such affordable prices. I can't wait to meet that man who fired Jollie. He must be a pretty big guy. I wonder how much money he makes."

It took them only ten minutes to get to Allmart.

There was no one to greet the ladies when they entered the store. Peppy was quick to point out the error.

"No greeting? No 'Welcome to Allmart'? Can you believe this, Leslie? I mean, can you believe this? I want to see a manager!" she said loudly.

When no one paid attention, she yelled, "I said—I want to see a manager now, or I go right over to To-Get and spend my money there, and I have a lot to spend! You better believe it!"

Two men in worn, shiny suits rushed over.

"Good morning, Miss. I am Mr. Smit, the manager." Mr. Smit made a short, courtly bow.

The other man corrected him. "No, I am the manager, Mr. Smit— your shift ended fifteen minutes ago. Good morning. I am Mr. Foote." He reached for a handshake, but Peppy left his sweaty paw hanging in the air.

"No, Mr. Foote. I believe your watch may be running fast or slow, whatever the case might be. I will handle this lady's complaint," said Mr. Smit.

Leslie was embarrassed and left to wander about the store.

"My complaint is this—your greeter seems to have deserted his post. I am accustomed to being welcomed," Peppy said angrily.

"Then let me welcome you," said Mr. Foote.

"No, I insist that I be the one to welcome this lady, Mr. Foote," said Mr. Smit.

Peppy pouted and then stomped. "Where is the regular welcomer? He was especially skilled at making me glad I came to Allmart."

"Um, he was let go, Miss?" said Mr. Foote.

"Let go! By whom? By whose authority?" Peppy folded her hands against her chest.

"That would be Mr. Pimpernel. He's in the employee lunchroom chatting, as is his custom. It's his day off, but he comes in anyway because he has neither family nor friends, so he has plenty of time to talk with you," said Mr. Smit. "I'll get him for you—a moment." *What could such a beautiful woman want with Jollie Inch or Buzzard Head?* he wondered. He hurried off to find Mr. Pimpernel.

Mr. Foote stood smiling foppishly at Peppy until she brought up Allmart's spring fashion line. He interrupted her by declaring, "Duty calls!" then fled the scene.

Not five minutes later, Mr. Smit came hurrying toward the entrance, followed by Mr. Pimpernel, who wore his usual black pants and safety-pinned coat.

"Good day, Miss. I am Mr. Pimpernel. You were inquiring about one of our ex-employees?" said Mr. Pimpernel, bobbing his bald head.

Peppy stared. "Why—why, you can't be Jollie's manager! You couldn't beat up anyone! You're just a runt!"

A man waiting in the long returns line was listening. He was a lawyer, a very lousy lawyer in dire need of work. He left the line to address Mr. Pimpernel.

"Mr. Pimpernel, I am here to represent the very employee this lady is referring to, the same employee that you assaulted and then dismissed from Allmart's employ, thus depriving him of his living. Did you follow the proper procedures to terminate this man? I will need several copies of the paperwork. He may be only one of many named in a class-action suit against Allmart. You, sir, will be personally named as the chief offender."

Mr. Pimpernel wiped his head with a napkin. He was too young to retire, too young to be so weary, and too young to be so old.

The man pressed on. "Sir, I am addressing you! Do you understand what I am saying? I will need your name, your contact information, and your social security number."

"Perhaps we were overeager in our rush to terminate Mr. Inch. Perhaps Allmart should reconsider." Mr. Pimpernel worried.

"I should say so! In fact, I suggest you also contact an attorney!" The man handed Peppy a business card and left.

Meanwhile, Leslie had taken a small notebook from her purse and was walking around, writing down prices and names of food. She hadn't realized that Allmart carried groceries and the low prices, even of brand names, astonished her. When she saw Peppy waving to her from the exit door, she hurried over to meet her. The two women tried to leave, but a man wearing a pinstriped navy blue suit, dark glasses and an ear bud snuck up behind Leslie and took her arm.

"May I speak with you, Miss?" he said. Another man, also wearing a pinstriped navy blue suit, dark glasses and an ear bud, appeared on the opposite side of the first man. He took Leslie's other arm. The two men walked Leslie toward the back of the store.

"Peppy, wait!" called out Leslie.

"Call me later and tell me what you bought!" Peppy called back in a friendly tone. She had recognized one of the men as a particularly bad date she'd had a few years back. As a favor to Leslie, Peppy asked Mr. Pimpernel to give her the lawyer's business card.

Leslie was terrified. The men took her into a dark, dusty room. The room was empty save for a table, a chair, and an old-fashioned black phone.

Although the phone rang intermittently, no one ever answered it, and Leslie jumped each time it sounded off.

"Young lady, we are obliged to identify ourselves as loss-prevention investigators employed by Allmart to watch for and detain low-down rotten thieves like yourself. Now, please remove your coat," one of the men said. He took Leslie's coat and began taking jewelry out of the pockets.

"That stuff's not mine!" exclaimed Leslie.

"It's your coat, isn't it? But you're right about the jewelry you ripped off—it's not yours, it's Allmart's. Are you ready to make a statement to the effect that you stole this merchandise?" the investigator asked.

"I swear that stuff isn't mine!" Leslie cried.

"Please give me your purse," the other investigator said.

Leslie handed him her purse. Inside were five lipsticks, an eye shadow, and seven tubes of mascara, all in their original packages.

The investigator removed the merchandise and closed the purse. "Looks like an open-and-shut case," he said sternly. "I'll call the police."

He made a copy of Leslie's driver license and walked out. Ten minutes passed. When he didn't come back, the other investigator went to find him. On his way out, he bumped into Mr. Pimpernel, who was listening outside the door.

"Excuse me, Pimp," he said. Loss-prevention investigators like to make up pet names. "Have you seen Charlie? He left the interrogation room to call the police. There's only me in there to guard the perpetrator."

"Hi, Howard. I just saw Charlie out front. He said he was going to lunch," said Mr. Pimpernel.

"That bastard!" the investigator swore. "Leaves me with all the paperwork. Well, screw him! I quit!"

Investigator Howard left the store. On the way home, he applied for a job at To-Get so he wouldn't have to work with Charlie anymore. Mr. Pimpernel went back to the employee lounge to recover from the ordeal. It was not his job to guard dangerous criminals.

When Charlie returned from lunch and found that his coworker had left, he went home because he didn't want to work with Howard anymore. Charlie also stopped at To-Get to apply for a job. To-Get had lots of shoplifters, and the store hired both men the following day.

Leslie waited an hour in Allmart's small, dusty room before she crept out. She actually passed the investigator who had gone to lunch, but he didn't notice her. The frightened woman wandered toward downtown and found a BART station. It took five stops and a transfer to get home. Leslie finally reached her bomb shelter. She slept badly that night.

The next morning, Mr. Pimpernel found the jewelry, makeup, and a copy of Leslie's driver's license on the table in the dark, dusty room. He called the police and two officers arrived a half hour later. They were the same height, and their faces were chiseled and handsome. One was blond and one was dark-haired.

"Thank goodness you're here, officers. An insane woman stole jewelry and makeup, and she threatened two of my employees, both of whom became so upset they had to leave work." Mr. Pimpernel gave the police a copy of Leslie's driver license and the items he had found in her purse and her coat.

"Don't worry, sir," said the blond officer. "We are professionals, and we will find the scofflaw."

"Justice—" said the dark-haired officer—"I promise you, justice will be done."

Leslie considered going to the police to turn herself in, but she had never been in trouble before. *But I didn't do anything*, she kept telling herself. She wished she had someone to talk to, but Peppy had deserted her at Allmart, Jollie and Jud Roy would only celebrate her troubles, and Dino was nuts. Leslie didn't know anyone else—except for Larger Billie. When she got to her apartment, she hesitated and then called.

"Larger Billie? Long time, no hear. Are you busy this—"

Larger Billie got two speeding tickets driving from Livermore to Oakland. It took him only a half an hour to locate the bomb shelter. He apologized to Leslie for being late, which he hadn't been since neither of them had mentioned his coming at all.

After losing Ye Olde Grocery for failing to keep up with ever-increasing government paperwork regulations, Larger Billie had taken a job managing Secureway, a large, conglomerate grocery store that employed nearly a thousand people just to complete forms. He made a lot more money than he had ever made being in business for himself. It was easier too, and they provided health insurance, something he had never had.

"Leslie—Leslie, my darling, how I've missed you. I'm here, Leslie, I'm here. Come back to Livermore, come back with me tonight. I'm losing weight—did you notice?"

"Go back to Livermore? Larger Billie, you must be kidding. I can't leave Oakland. There's my job at the library, and did I tell you I'm going to be in a play? It's at eight thirty next week on March 17, St. Patrick's Day, at Millard Fillmore Elementary-Adult Education. Besides, I hate Livermore. My mother's there, and it's just—oh, Larger, it's just I don't know what to do! I've never been in trouble before, and I could—I could go to jail!"

"Jail!" Larger Billie was shocked.

"Larger, I'm in trouble—big trouble. But I didn't do anything!"

"What is it you didn't do?" His big arms squeezed her petite body.

"It was Peppy's fault. We went to Allmart and somehow she put make-up and jewelry in my purse, and I got arrested for shoplifting. Peppy wasn't even near me. But it had to be her. It had to be."

"Who's Peppy? And why would she do such a thing?"

"Peppy's in my writing class. A group of us are putting on a play we wrote for the PTA. Oh, Larger, has it been so long since we've talked?" she mumbled into his armpit. "Larger, I can't breathe."

Large Billie loosened his grip. "Leslie! That's great. You made some friends."

His compliment made her feel ashamed—Leslie Tomatiny, the woman who finally made a friend. *Why should Peppy have everything? I want to be Peppy. Oh God, make me be Peppy.*

Her blue eyes met Larger Billie's brown ones.

"There's only one reason I can think of that would make her do such a thing—jealousy. She wanted to go to Allmart to get Jollie's job back. And she's mad at Jud Roy because he's dumping her. Also, she's interested in Bottomly. But he wants me too!" Leslie could hardly believe what she was saying. *A thief...and now a liar,* she thought.

Larger Billie scratched his temple. "Who are Jollie, Jud Roy, and Bottomly?"

"Men. They're men, Larger. Those three men are—well, they're crazy about me. We all became friends, and they preferred me to Peppy, and Peppy got mad and put stuff in my pockets and my purse." *What am I saying?* Leslie asked herself.

Larger hung his head. *Those men are probably all thinner than I am. I'm losing her—I always knew she was too good for me.*

Although their reunion was awkward, Leslie and Larger spent the night together anyways. The two held one another innocently until they fell asleep in Leslie's soft, warm bed, their heads resting peacefully on sachet-scented pillows.

He was frisky the following morning, and Leslie asked him to leave. *The bomb shelter isn't large enough for Larger Billie,* she told herself. *Besides, what would people say? Her and a fat man—two losers.*

"But he's good to me," she whispered to herself. "In every way."

"Yeah," said Jollie from the cloud. "He was good to her."

CHAPTER 25

Dino and Leslie

● ● ●

LESLIE WENT TO CLASS THAT evening, but she barely spoke. She was on her way to the kindergarten room for the usual meeting with The Three Musketeers when Dino stepped out from behind a building and blocked her path.

"Leslie Tomatiny, a moment of your time. Leslie Tomatiny, do not ask how I know, but two federal agents, one of whom dated Peppy Zipline several months ago, arrested you yesterday for shoplifting at Allmart."

Leslie gasped. "Agents? You can't mean—you mean that those men at Allmart work for the FBI?"

Dino sounded urgent. "I cannot say. I suspect you are the reincarnation of some desperate outlaw who died without suffering the consequences of his evil deeds. You have taken on his evil disposition and others will hunt and hate you until you suffer the punishment you and your fore- and future bearers deserve. You may choose to commit a large crime and suffer horribly but get it over with in one shot or commit several small crimes and suffer mildly but frequently. I always suggest doing the smaller crimes with mild, frequent suffering. The crimes are easier to come across and more enjoyable to commit—eating fast food, drinking boxed wine, being rude to people and pissing them off—with this last one, you can score big by getting your ass kicked by a stranger. Leslie Tomatiny, let me help you. I am available tomorrow at two o'clock. Because of our close friendship, I will conduct your séance for only fifty dollars, cash only."

This is ridiculous, thought Leslie. But she was scared. She needed some-one to talk to, someone not as frisky as Larger Billie, and Dino seemed to be the only one who was the least bit interested in Leslie's troubles.

"Dino? Can I pay you twenty-five dollars now and twenty-five dollars later?"

"Leslie Tomatiny, be at my sanctuary tomorrow at two o'clock."

Leslie considered.

"OK, well, maybe I'll come by."

"Until tomorrow then," Dino said. She gazed into Leslie's face and saw the deep sadness that was Leslie's stock in trade.

Dino's sessions took place in her home. She'd arranged the shabby, single apartment for maximum effect. A dark, gloomy light for contacting the dead or anything else a client might think up hid the filthy rug and the cheap, plastic beanbags Dino referred to as "sacred meditation pillows."

When Leslie arrived at Dino's apartment, Dino answered the door wearing a skimpy belly dancer's costume and a filmy, almost-see-through dress.

"Welcome, Leslie Tomatiny. You are admiring my spirit skin." Dino intoned, "I must be free of vain hindrances when I speak to the gods. When I am alone, I contact the mystics naked. They respond more will-ingly when I present my nether regions.

"Uh, forget about it, Dino. I'm straight as an arrow," Leslie said nervously.

"Do not fear, Leslie Tomatiny. I am sexless." Dino looked disappointed.

Leslie entered the sanctuary, and Dino instructed her to tiptoe past electric tea lights (for fire safety) and sit down in a particular sacred medi-tation beanbag chair, chosen especially for her. There was even a sticker on it that said "Leslie Tomatiny."

Dino sat in a comfortable Lazy Boy recliner across from Leslie and leaned forward.

"Leslie Tomatiny, I will implore the gods on your behalf. I will con-nect you with Hagos, who specializes in reforming misguided dregs who steal other people's stuff."

Leslie looked around, and then winced. About five feet from the sacred beanbag chair, a huge cat with glowing green eyes perched on a cat tower and stared down at her. The cat was a pet Dino had as a child. When it died, her parents had it stuffed and presented it to their distraught daughter. The taxidermist had been a master, and it looked beautifully alive.

"Leslie Tomatiny, I bid you now to concentrate. I bid you to lean back into your sacred meditation chair. Study the cat carefully. Do not look away from its eyes or the magical connection will not take place."

When Leslie was comfortably staring into the dead animal's glassy eyes, Dino slipped behind a curtain. She banged a gong and shook a caged chicken that clucked and flapped about. A timer went off. The hoot of a thousand owls floated in from another hidden speaker. Bats flapped. Whales mourned. Monkeys chattered, and someone far in the distance yodeled a Christmas carol.

Then Dino spoke through the cat, whose skull housed a tiny speaker.

"Do not permit your ears to leave my voice. The connection is as delicate as a single strand of a spider's web. I am the last reincarnation of the woman Hagos, born in Ethiopia multiple millions of years ago. The top gods reincarnated me so many times, that they ran out of living things to put me in, and I became Hagos, the Goddess Who Dwells in a Cat's Mouth. I, Hagos know you, Leslie Tomatiny. I know every lineage of your every reincarnation. I see mud huts, a fruit gatherer, a single-celled organism—keep staring into my eyes, Leslie Tomatiny. I, Hagos, will contact your personal spiritual advisors so that they may determine how you can surmount and conquer the justifiable guilt that so tortures you in this time of great need that robs you of your sleep and releases the monster from the closet of your mind and feasts—"

"Uh, this really isn't working for me," Leslie said, interrupting.

"And feasts on your eyes and robs you of sleep—"

"You said that already, Dino," Leslie said.

"That stare up at the sky, that—"

"Uh, how long is this going to last?" Leslie asked.

"Stare into my eyes—I am Hagos—"

"Yeah, I know, Hagos the long-winded Ethiopian reincarnation in the guise of a dead cat," said Leslie.

"Concentrate on my eyes," said Hagos.

"Dino, I'm leaving. This isn't helping. You can forget the fifty bucks."

"Leslie Tomatiny, have you hurt someone recently?" Dino asked. "Perhaps caused someone pain?"

Leslie thought of Larger Billie.

"Okay—you got me. I hurt Larger Billie. He was always kind to me, and he gave me so many raises. I was making more money than people who had worked for him for twenty years," confessed Leslie.

"Leslie Tomatiny, I knew this to be true. Hagos tells me it is not your shoplifting habit that grieves you, but your love for this man. I bid you concentrate on Hagos's eyes."

Leslie sniffed back a tear and concentrated on Hagos's frozen eyes. Five minutes passed, and then ten, and then a full fifteen minutes before Hagos spoke, again in the voice of Dino, who was still acting as portal.

"I see a face rising out of the mist over a bog. The bog cannot be seen. It runs under a tree, the tree is hidden in a deep forest, the forest is forgotten by the people who once lived near there, in a now abandoned town, on the outskirts of a city that is no longer populated."

Dino kept an outdated phone book, which was an essential element to her work as a mystic.

"The spiritual advisors of your cult are here. A face speaks to me in syllables, it says, 'Call me Jackson, comma, Frank D., of Little Rock. I am head spokesperson of the cult. Also, we have your distant relative Kelley, comma, T.'

"'Good evening to you, Leslie Tomatiny,'" Kelley, T. said. "'I am the Standing Grand Magee of your cult. Allow me to introduce my vice-grandee, from Istanbul, Langly, comma, B.'

"'Pleasure to meet you, Leslie Tomatiny. Sorry you can't meet all of us; there's about three thousand family members here. Wait, Leslie Tomatiny! I see something. A man—a round man with a large heart who loves you very much. Green vegetables and cuts of meat float in the air and circle around his head. Does this mean anything to you?'"

"It must be Larger Billie. He is hugely overweight, and his heart is probably large due to obesity," said Leslie.

"'A large man with a large heart,'" said Kelly, T. "'Leslie, once upon a time in the future, I see you and this man meeting in the afterlife. He will have been waiting many years to greet you. You and he will have taken the form of ladybugs, and the two of you will live in the Tibetan wilderness, where pesticides are never used. In this relationship, you and your partner will fly happily through produce, and you will have every opportunity to beg his forgiveness. He will live on healthy green vegetables and lose much weight, so things should be a lot more pleasant for you.'"

"It wasn't unpleasant. He was so gentle and considerate. He was good to me," said Leslie.

"'I think what Kelly, comma, T. is saying is that if you don't want to bother with the fat man now, you can always wait until you're both ladybugs,'" Langley, B. said. "We'll all understand."

"I'm not so sure I want to wait," insisted Leslie. "Larger Billie even asked me to live with him."

"Leslie Tomatiny, the dead are never wrong," Dino announced. She clapped her hands, turned on the lights, and collected her fee. "Another appointment?"

"No," said Leslie. "It was an interesting experiment, but I still think it's bullshit. See you in class."

The good-bye hug Dino gave her surprised Leslie. Then, Leslie, she did something she should have done years ago. She cried—first a single tear and then another, until a wash of salty comfort ran down her face. Leslie leaned against Dino awkwardly, wishing it would end. When she finally stopped, Leslie was too embarrassed to say anything. She went home and spent the evening huddled in her bed. The following afternoon, she wrote a poem that she very much wanted to share.

Jollie always clutched his cloud during that particular scene. Being dead, he couldn't cry, but he always imagined doing so.

The next evening, the classroom was full. Leslie breathed in the yeasty warmth of other human beings. It was comforting, and she audibly sighed before taking her seat. She avoided looking at either Peppy or Dino. Jollie was absent.

Jud Roy welcomed her back to class. "Ah! Welcome back, Leslie. It was damn inconsiderate of you to ditch the last class and walk away from the play. Do you have something to read today?"

Leslie cleared her throat and read her poem.

Funeral for Justice

Justice gasped, and breathed its last.
No one came to mourn its past.
Dead by unnamed circumstance,
Strangled by hard evidence,
And facts and talk and money spent,
Till Justice lost its confidence,
And every juror cast his vote
On which attorney better spoke,
Then in a dream I did but see
A fat man watching over me.

"Comments?" asked Jud Roy. There were none.

Leslie stared at her paper. She gave Dino a hard look and ran out of the classroom.

"Meeting's at seven!" Jud Roy cheerfully called to the fleeing woman.

Leslie found a restroom and sat down on the tiny kindergarten toilet. The childish atmosphere soothed her. A half hour later, she felt well enough to leave the soft, dark room and go to the meeting.

CHAPTER 26

The Play Progresses Nicely

● ● ●

THE PLAY WAS PROGRESSING NICELY. Each Musketeer had written his or her own part, and Jud Roy combined them into a grammatically correct theater experience. They'd almost finished the entire thing. However, there were some complaints.

Dino was disturbed about the size of her part. "Three Musketeers, I am playing two roles, challenging ones, but I am hardly on stage. Jud Roy Lebowitz, you tease the audience with promises and then do not deliver the best that I have to offer."

"Dino, you're fat and weird as all hell," Jud Roy explained. "Too damn weird to be in a play or even a book! That's why your part is smaller than any of the others."

Before Dino could answer, Jollie jumped up and began pacing back and forth. "I am shocked—I say, shocked—that I do not have a larger speaking part. I play a world-renowned football quarterback at the height of my career, in the arms of my love and the throes of death. I wrote fifteen full pages of dialogue for my character. Where are they now? Anyone could understand why Dino should have a small part, but as the lead, I should be on stage throughout the entire play—and of course, the lead always goes home with the best-looking woman."

He looked at Peppy, who looked at Jud Roy, who looked away.

Jud Roy answered back, "Look, Jollie—first off, if I had another quarterback, you wouldn't even be in the play, and second, if we had included all your crappy dialogue, the thing would have stunk to high hell and there wouldn't be time for anyone else to say anything. God, I should have bested you that night at Burgers and Booze."

Jollie's nostrils flared. "Bested me, a quarterback? Unlikely. You wouldn't even be here if I hadn't kept my temper. Uncivilized buffoon! Don't you even think of threatening me. I'll go straight to Bottomly. I'll go to his office every day until you're fired, as well you should be."

Jud Roy started to say something about Jollie's mother and stopped himself. He shrugged his shoulders. "You're probably right, Jollie— Bottomly would fire me. Besides, we need you. I can't take away everyone's lines, but you can be on stage through the entire play. Yes, I insist. Without you, it would flop for sure."

"Agreed," Jollie said.

Peppy and Jud Roy were satisfied with their parts. Their roles made up the majority of the play. Leslie didn't really care how long she would be on stage. She still feared the police would show up and arrest her. She didn't give a damn about anything else.

As promised, Jud Roy made the necessary changes so that Jollie was always on stage. It was hard to believe, but if everyone could stand one another for the next few weeks, the show would go on.

No one except for the PTA ever used the dusty old auditorium they would perform in, because it was moldy and falling apart. The park across the street from the school had a very nice, new recreation room that Millard Fillmore could use, and at a reasonable price too. However, the school board refused to pay to rent the recreation room for PTA meetings because only about half of the members ever showed up.

Jollie was doing exercises in the cloud fluff as he watched. Exercise in cloud fluff mostly involved struggling to stand up, falling down, and then doing it all over again.

All five of the Three Musketeers loved being on stage, even Leslie. Peppy wore a short skirt that rode up, and sat in the front on a wooden box. Jud Roy stood near one side, where he could watch everyone; Dino stood on the opposite side and stared into space. Jollie lay on a bed in the center of the stage, and Leslie sat hunched in a corner in the back. Mr. Bottomly often stopped by—he always sat in the front row of the audience, where he could look up Peppy's skirt.

Leslie's acting talent came as a surprise, especially to her. She even impressed Jud Roy. "That's perfect, Leslie. Just keep in the back, in the corner there for as long as you can. That's great—you really know how to make a pathetic character look pathetic. Dino, you're on—try not to slump."

Dino walked back and forth on the stage in front of the others and read from a stapled stack of papers.

"Parent Teacher Association—my name is Dino Quiet Room. I am sure the topic of tonight's play will please you. Our play is about death, specifically the death of our hero, Quarterback Rufus Dandelion, the most admired man in any football game or locker room. Be ready for haunting performances, sweeping drama, and a nightmare that will horrify even the bravest of you. I bid you sit back, relax, and enjoy *Death of a Quarterback*."

"Stop! Don't you think you should introduce the actors? Or at perhaps only the lead?" asked Jollie.

"We'll introduce everyone or no one at all!" yelled Jud Roy.

"I introduced myself," said Dino.

"Do you really think that a play about death is an appropriate topic for the PTA meeting?" asked Mr. Bottomly.

"There's a love story in it between the philandering doctor and a crazy woman," said Peppy.

"Love—it's something I can never resist," said Mr. Bottomly, trying to catch Peppy's eye with his normal one.

Jud Roy turned to Mr. Bottomly. "Thank you for coming in, Superintendent Bottomly. We have a lot of rehearsing to do yet. Please stop by again."

The play was only ten days away.

CHAPTER 27

Superintendent Bottomly Gets Frisky

● ● ●

SUPERINTENDENT BOTTOMLY SAT IN HIS office, chewing on a pencil. He had nothing to do, and he had been spending hours every day thinking about Peppy. Over and over he told himself, *Consorting with a woman is inappropriate and unbecoming to the position of superintendent, especially a superintendent who is a former military man. Time to stop daydreaming about past glories. A superintendent must have his wits about him.*

But no matter how often he promised himself he would stop, he would call Peppy's number three or four times a day and hang up when she answered the phone.

That afternoon, he made an uncharacteristic fifth call and waited for her to speak.

"Dick!" she shouted into the phone, and hung up.

The sweet sound of her voice inspired Mr. Bottomly to make a sixth call. This time, he spoke. "This is not Dick. I am calling for Ms. Peppy Zipline."

"So, you finally decided to talk! I know exactly who you are. You're Miguel, the busboy who's been following me around night and day." Peppy thought a moment, then continued. "I've called the police three times already, and they've been watching your house. They're on the way this very minute to arrest you. You'll not only end up getting fired from Pancake Heaven but you'll be deported back to Mexico!"

Mr. Bottomly caught a glimpse of himself in the window. He was really beginning to like the patch over his eye. It gave him rakish confidence. "Take a hold of yourself, little lady. You have me mistaken for somebody else. I am Superintendent Bob Bottomly, and I have not been calling and hanging up on you every day. I have never disrespected a woman, nor any other female. And I have certainly never worked in a kitchen or been to Mexico. Ha ha! The very idea. I'm calling about an urgent matter."

"Oh—excuse me, Mr. Superintendent. I'm forever getting phone calls from a desperate busboy who cannot seem to forget that we had a brief tryst while he was washing dishes. Were you calling to ask me out?"

"Why—why, Peppy, my dear. Whatever did I do to arouse such suspicion? No, no—I just wanted to tell you—my office is always open should Jud Roy bother you again."

Peppy remembered their previous conversation about France and Mr. Bottomly's family connections. "Thank you, Mr., I mean, Superintendent Bottomly. You are a true gentleman. It's surprising how some men will treat an honest woman. Thank you so much."

"Such behavior on the part of a professor must cause you much pain. Sometimes an evening with an understanding friend in a quiet restaurant helps."

"Great idea! I was just thinking about going out for a good, strong drink."

"I don't approve of women drinking alcohol—it makes them have sex with strangers." Mr. Bottomly frowned.

"But I'll be with you, and you're not a stranger!" Peppy exclaimed. "Do you know the Hoegaarden? They have very good specialty cocktails."

"The bar with the topless women?" asked Mr. Bottomly. He had heard of it but had never been there. To be seen in such a place by the head of the school board could destroy him.

"The police made them stop the topless thing. But it's 'Bring Your Baby to the Bar' night, so a baby gets you half off drinks, and it includes well drinks with house liquor."

Peppy wanted Mr. Bottomly to know the drinks were cheap. It wasn't likely, but he might not pay. Jud Roy had burned her once, and at the Dead Lobster too, where drinks were expensive.

"I wasn't aware you had children," said Mr. Bottomly warmly.

"No, I just bring a doll. If anyone looks at me suspicious-like, I just pop out a boob. No one seems to mind."

Mr. Bottomly was silent for a moment. "I suppose a woman must at times give in to her maternal desires. As I said, ordinarily, I do not approve of women drinking, but since I will be there to insure your safety, I will make an exception. I've driven by the Hoegaarden many times. I'll meet you there at O twelve hundred. That's six o'clock, civilian time."

"Uh, OK." Peppy hung up and rushed to her closet to select what to wear. *Maybe Mr. Bottomly wouldn't be so bad. Besides, he just might buy me a good dinner.*

Mr. Bottomly was early, and Peppy was late. The bar was full of healthy, crying babies and tired, harried parents. Busy bartenders rushed to serve the customers and wipe up the drinks the babies had spilled. When Peppy walked in, Mr. Bottomly was eagerly watching for her from an obscure booth in the corner. He adjusted his eye patch and rose to greet her.

"My dear!" he said, taking her arm in a firm grip. "I rather expected you to be on time, but I will overlook it for such a beautiful lady. I have a lovely table over here." Mr. Bottomly led her to the booth and waited for her to sit down before sitting down himself.

Peppy had to yell over the noise. "Mr. Superintendent, it's so nice to see you again!" Peppy was carrying a plastic doll with curly red hair, the same shade as hers.

The superintendent yelled back, "My, what a beautiful baby! It's about dinnertime; the poor lamb must be hungry. Ha ha! You can see I like to have a good time." Mr. Bottomly leaned forward and stared hopefully at Peppy's breasts.

"Perhaps a sherry?" Mr. Bottomly hollered.

"Bourbon, straight up—with a lime and a cherry," screamed Peppy.

"Waiter! Your attention, waiter!" Mr. Bottomly yelled to a cocktail server. She didn't hear him. 'Bring Your Baby to the Bar' night was always extremely noisy, what with all the crying parents and babies.

Peppy leaned in toward Mr. Bottomly. "Tell me about France," she shouted. "Is it wonderful?"

"Wee. Oh, yes. Paris is one of the most beautiful cities in the world. To walk along the Chumps de Elyse on a spring morning is to be in heaven itself," Mr. Bottomly shouted back. "Two bourbons, straight up. Make mine a double," he shouted to a waiter who paused near their table.

He took Peppy's hand and stared with his one eye into her lovely face. Peppy admired how the eye patch made him look like a pirate.

"While we wait for your drink, dear lady, we can either talk about Professor Jud Roy's conduct or the despicable behavior of other uncivilized men," hollered Mr. Bottomly.

"The behavior of uncircumcised men?" shouted Peppy.

The bar was getting louder. The babies outnumbered the adults, and now, even the waiters were crying and swearing. Conversation was impossible.

As soon as Peppy tossed down her drink, Mr. Bottomly suggested that they go somewhere quieter. She agreed, so long as it wasn't Burgers and Booze, Allmart, or the bowling alley. Mr. Bottomly walked her to his car. When Peppy tried to open the door, he blocked her and opened it for her, firmly taking her arm as he did so. As they drove off, the wailing of babies faded away behind them.

"Where are we going?" Peppy asked.

Mr. Bottomly suggested they go to his condominium. "Flower, you seem to be particularly interested in France. I have three lovely prints I would very much like to show you, all by the French artist Edouard Manet, and all framed and covered with glass. I have the famous "Olympia," a watercolor of a naked prostitute reclining on a couch and the equally famous "Luncheon on the Grass," which depicts two well-dressed men picnicking with two oddly placed naked women. Additionally, I have a very rare print, Edouard Manet's lesser known "Blonde with Bare Breasts," a watercolor of a blond woman with bare breasts. My condominium is very close by. As I said before, I do not approve of women drinking, but our being together makes this a special occasion. I always keep a fully stocked bar, which, that is, which includes, I mean to say, that the bar is ample with maraschino cherries, limes, olives, pickled onions, citrus twists, orange juice, coconut milk, strawberries, and pineapple. I also have bourbon and tequila.

Peppy loved the bar selection. "OK," she said. Mr. Bottomly took a sharp left into a handsome condominium building and expertly glided the car into a garage.

"Wow," said Peppy. "We were right in front of your apartment building."

"Condominium," Mr. Bottomly corrected her.

Again, Mr. Bottomly opened the car door, took her arm, and guided her to his condo.

Mr. Bottomly had quite a nice place. "What a lovely apartment!" Peppy exclaimed.

"Condominium," Mr. Bottomly corrected her.

"Is it rent-controlled?" asked Peppy.

"No, I own it," said Mr. Bottomly.

"Wow!" Peppy exclaimed. "You mean you own this whole building?"

"I was going to show you my Manet etchings," Mr. Bottomly reminded her.

"Oh, yes," said Peppy. "The pictures."

"Behold," said Mr. Bottomly, throwing his arm out toward three prints on the living room wall. Peppy looked at the Manet prints. "French women are sure ugly," she said.

Mr. Bottomly raised his eyebrows. "Perhaps you see them as unattractive because you are so beautiful. The French are in fact a most attractive and interesting people. I met quite a few during my tours there with the navy. They have quite a well-deserved reputation for romance—for romance quite different from the Puritan, Victorian kind they practice in England."

"I met an ambassador from England," said Peppy. "I met him in San Francisco, not Scandinavia, though. He said he was a spy."

"A spy? I knew several in the navy. My dear, why don't I put on a little music to set the mood?" The superintendent chose a CD from a rack on the wall. "This is a particular favorite of mine." The room filled with a rousing military march. Mr. Bottomly saluted Peppy, raced up the stairs, and returned with a laundry basket of sheets.

Mr. Bottomly gave Peppy a flat, commanding look from his one eye. "My dear, I don't mean to be rude, but I have neglected to fold my laundry. Probably because of my strict military training, I simply cannot abide wrinkled sheets. Would you mind helping me fold them?"

"I guess not," Peppy said. She rather liked the fresh smell of clean laundry.

Mr. Bottomley sensed some interest. "When I was a young sailor in France, I learned many things. Interestingly enough, the French fold sheets together in the nude. It's a way of showing trust and is sometimes used by disagreeing politicians. As long as we have these unfolded sheets, we might as well try it—by way of experimentation."

"Trust and folding sheets," Peppy said. "It makes sense, doesn't it?"

"Yes, my dear—I think you are in need of someone to trust. I feel your sadness and need."

Mr. Bottomly pulled down the blinds and began removing his clothes. Peppy hesitated. "Understand, Flower, that I give you these orders to protect you. The importance of following orders cannot be overstated. Remember that I am a superintendent with prior military experience. You are perfectly safe," Mr. Bottomly assured her.

Peppy nodded her assent and removed her clothes. Safe sounded promising.

Mr. Bottomly stood back a moment to admire her lithe body and perfect skin.

"And now, for the sheets," he cried. Reverently, he lifted one from the laundry basket.

Mr. Bottomly took two corners of one side of a sheet and Peppy took two corners of the other side. They both extended their arms.

"Slowly, slowly," said Mr. Bottomly in a hushed, murky voice.

Peppy began folding the sheet in half.

Mr. Bottomly became frantic. "Slower, slower!" insisted. "Follow my lead!"

"Yes, Superintendent," said Peppy. She was all a-tremble.

Gently, carefully, Mr. Bottomly and Peppy brought their hands up and folded the sheet in half. Mr. Bottomly reached down and grabbed the lower corner of his side of the sheet, and Peppy did the same on the other side. Together, they raised up the four corners, so that the sheet stretched between them.

"Again! Slowly!" cried Mr. Bottomly, and they folded the sheet into fourths.

"Now," Mr. Bottomly commanded softly, "walk toward me. With grace, woman, with grace!"

In a quiet, syncretized motion, Peppy walked toward Mr. Bottomly for a third fold. Their bodies pressed against each other, separated only by the cool, sweet-smelling sheet. The nearness of him! She pressed against him harder.

"To reach the bottom of the sheet for the next fold, you must bow down, as though you were worshiping me," instructed Mr. Bottomly. Peppy did so.

"Take the corners—give them to me now!" Mr. Bottomly ordered.

Peppy bent lower and took the corners of the sheet. She walked forward to Mr. Bottomly and gave up the corners willingly, even gratefully.

"Now kneel down!" Mr. Bottomly commanded. He put the sheet over Peppy's head. Peppy took the hint and proceeded.

After some minutes, Mr. Bottomly removed the sheet from Peppy's head. Mr. Bottomly studied the sheet carefully. "It will not do," he said, and frowned at Peppy before throwing it on the floor. The superintendent closed his eyes and took a long, deep breath. "Again!" he commanded, and took a second sheet out of the basket. This time, it was a fitted sheet, and especially challenging. Peppy bit her lips.

It took two hours for them to fold a single sheet to Mr. Bottomly's expectations and, by that time, Peppy was so tired, she fell asleep on the floor among the piles of rejected linen. Mr. Bottomly slept in his bed.

CHAPTER 28

The Play and How It Happened in Spite of Jud Roy's Script

● ● ●

JOLLIE'S EFFORTS AT ALLMART BROUGHT in the entire membership of the PTA and nearly one hundred Allmart shoppers. In fact, there were so many people, they ran out of chairs and latecomers had to stand up in the back. Mr. Bottomly congratulated himself on the success of his idea to provide entertainment. It was only six o'clock, but Jud Roy, Leslie, Dino, and Peppy were already waiting backstage. Jollie was milling about the room, studying the people as they came in.

A man and woman, obviously new to the PTA meetings, stood apart, watching the rest of the people. Seeing that Jollie was alone, they went over and introduced themselves and then politely asked if he had any children in the school.

Jollie glanced down at the man's freckled, tiny head and sneered, "No, I certainly do not have children in this nor any other school. My name is Jollie Inch. I am a thespian, and this meeting is to conclude with the premiere of my latest work, a play, which I both wrote and star in—yes, Jollie Inch. It's an old family name. I was named for my deceased father—a great, great man. I'm sure you've heard of him. No? Funny, the name is usually recognized, but of course, most of the events I appear at are attended only by artists like myself. Sh!" And here he lifted a warning finger and wagged it in the woman's face. "Say nothing! Paparazzi follow me everywhere."

The meeting was starting. Jollie nodded his head and then dashed off to join his fellow actors backstage.

Mr. Bottomly walked out from behind the curtain and took center stage. His large head was squeezed into a plastic green hat, and he wore the patch over his eye. Five grave people sat behind him on folding chairs. He addressed the audience.

"Welcome—welcome, parents and teachers of the PTA—and others. I am Robert Bottomly, Superintendent of Millard Fillmore Elementary-Adult Education. I should say I am the *District* Superintendent of the Millard Fillmore School. Yes, my name is Superintendent Bob Bottomly, Mr. Robert Bottomly if you will, but I invite you to call me Bob. In the navy, the sailors called me Bob the Swab, and the women called me—well, they just called me."

Here he gave a weak smile.

"Please welcome our PTA president, Ms., err, our PTA president and our four PTA officers—well, five PTA officers, four officers plus one, counting the president—please welcome our five PTA officers."

A few of the PTA members dribbled applause. Mr. Bottomly smiled and continued talking.

"We have a very special program tonight. As we all know, today is Saint Patrick's Day, so may I just say top of the morning!—and thank you for being here tonight instead of in some bar getting tanked. Before we begin the business and the purpose of our meeting, Ms. Penny's second-grade class will delight us with a performance of 'Oh Danny Boy,' also known as 'Londonderry Aire.'"

"I had no idea they called 'O Danny Boy' 'London Derriere,'" whispered a man to his wife.

"I was surprised myself. What can be the meaning of it?" whispered his wife.

"Perhaps Danny Boy had a girlfriend in London named London Derriere that he stopped by to see on his way to fight the war," said her husband.

"She must not have been a very nice lady," someone said.

"What war was that?" asked someone else. "Ireland and London, you know, they always fight the same wars."

"I wonder why," a woman said.

"The song doesn't say what war. But they played a pipe and called Old Danny Boy to go, and he left his own father alone to die," said a voice in the back.

"Sh! Fisheye's looking at us!" someone warned.

The superintendent frowned at the talkers. "Now—if I can have your attention—and I am not adverse nor objectionable to writing names on the chalkboard behind me—if I can direct your attention, Ms. Penny's class will sing, 'O Danny Boy.'"

Superintendent Bottomly's threat worried the audience, and they settled down. Everyone watched as he picked his seat. When the superintendent at last sat down, Ms. Penny led a crooked string of excited children out from behind the stage. Each child carried a cardboard square with a letter on it. When the children lined up in front of the stage, the letters spelled as follows:

HPAPY ST. PATCRIK'S AYD

Ms. Penny faced the children and raised her hand. They waited, dizzy with anticipation. Ms. Penny's hand came down and then made a sweeping motion.

Old Danny Boy
Thu Pipes Thu Pipes,
Um, a-all-ing
Again mmm, gain.
Fall Down, ummm Sky,
Duh Sun is all,
An all duy sun is Dy-ay-ing—

The children shuffled and giggled, and strained to reach the famously impossible notes by competitive screeching. By the end of the song, their little faces were red with exertion. The audience applauded, and the delighted kids smiled and looked adorable. They ran out, with Ms. Penny chasing after them, calling their names.

When it quieted down, Mr. Bottomly again took the stage. "Wonderful...wonderful. Thank you, Ms. Penny. Thank you, children. Now, let's get down to business and the hard work ahead. The required quorum is present, so the meeting can proceed."

Parents and teachers who did not know what a quorum was shifted in their squeaky chairs and peeked sideways at one another.

A man raised his hand. "This required forum," he asked, "is it a Roman theater?"

"I suppose it could be described as that," answered Mr. Bottomly. "This quorum or forum, if you will, this *required* quorum, I mean to say, indeed bases its principles on Roman democracy, something upon which I'm sure we can all agree on. I myself have traced my lineage to a eunuch slave boy who bathed Julius Caesar. Ms. Laura Lee, our PTA treasurer, bears responsibility for this large forum and is to be congratulated. Please congratulate our treasurer, Ms. Laura Lee."

Mr. Bottomly turned and smiled at a crooked woman in an ugly black dress. He sat down and a man in striped green pants took his place and began reading numbers from an accounting ledger.

The audience passed the time thinking about which bars it might be possible to get into on St. Patrick's Day. The children slept, the board looked stern, and all the activity made the meeting go by quickly and without incident.

When Mr. Bottomly once more took center stage, everyone hoped that it signified the end of the meeting. Mr. Bottomly beamed. "Honored PTA members, we have five very special guests here tonight. Jud Roy Lebowitz, *Professor* Jud Roy Lebowitz, is a published author whose work is read throughout the world—throughout the world, mind you, in countries that do not even speak English, if you can imagine such a thing. In spite of his notoriety, Professor Lebowitz is a modest man who writes under a podium, a *pseudonym* rather, but I can tell you that the title of one of his novels ends in *Dick*. He teaches creative writing, and he and his top four students have written and will perform for you now their play entitled *Death of a Quarterback*."

Mr. Bottomly adjusted his hat and walked down the steps of the stage to his seat in the front row. None of the PTA members wanted to stay, but they all did because they were afraid of what everyone else would think if they left.

Leslie passed out programs.

DEATH! OF A QUARTERBACK

Jollie Inch, starring as.........Quarterback Rufus Dandelion
Jud Roy Lebowitz, costarring as.........A Doctor
Peppy Zipline.........Rufus Dandelion's beautiful wife and the Doctor's beautiful girlfriend
Leslie Tomatiny.........Rufus Dandelion's plain girlfriend
Dino Quiet Room.........Moderator and the Grim Reaper

Copyright © 2015 [Jud Roy Lebowitz et al. the other actors.] All Rights Reserved.

When Leslie finished, Dino walked out from backstage.

INT. SCHOOL AUDITORIUM /
STAGE, CURTAINS CLOSED
MODERATOR and GRIM REAPER / DINO
(Center Stage)

MODERATOR and GRIM REAPER / DINO wears a long black cape, on which she has pinned a huge paper shamrock. She carries a feathered cane.

Ladies and Gentlemen, esteemed PTA President, Vice President, Superintendent, Treasurer, Secretary, Council Delegates, and Committee Chairs—the professor of the Millard Fillmore Creative Writing Class—Professor and Author Jud Roy Lebowitz and four of his most talented students have written and will perform a play for your delight and entertainment. When I say play, I say so in all modesty, for this piece has gained considerable notoriety and may soon be showing at the Triceratops Theater in San Francisco.

Jollie Inch will play Quarterback Rufus Dandelion. Jud Roy Lebowitz will play Rufus Dandelion's doctor. The beautiful Peppy Zipline will play Rufus Dandelion's wife and the Doctor's girlfriend. Leslie Tomatiny will play Rufus Dandelion's girlfriend. I, Dino Quiet Room, am your humble moderator and the only woman in the play who is not a wife or girlfriend. I will also play the Grim Reaper and other parts as assigned.

I now present to you—*dramatically*: *Death!—of a Quarterback*. Our play begins in a quiet hospital room. If you listen carefully, you can hear a low mumbling. It sounds flat and dreary and tells of boredom and emptiness of heart.

(Exits stage)

PTA AUDIENCE mumbles, indicating boredom and emptiness of heart. Several people cough as DOCTOR and MRS. DANDELION pull the rope that parts the dusty stage curtains.

INT. DESERTED HOSPITAL ROOM—AFTERNOON
RUFUS DANDELION lies under a white sheet on a hospital bed, cleverly represented by a pillow, a blanket, and a classroom table. A red licorice whip with one end taped to a water bottle tied to a coat rack and the other end taped to the stuffed arm substituted for an IV. Various bandages and empty aspirin bottles are scattered on a small table next to the bed.

MRS. DANDELION / PEPPY
(Whispers to doctor from behind the curtain)
The effect is fine.

SOMEONE IN THE AUDIENCE
I think he's moving, so he's not dead.

SOMEONE ELSE IN THE AUDIENCE
Is he supposed to be?
Rufus / Jollie sits up and turns so that he faces the audience. He wears a hospital gown and a red Hermes tie.

DOCTOR / JUD ROY
(From behind the curtain)
What the hell!

RUFUS / JOLLIE
Good evening, ladies and gentlemen and esteemed members of the PTA. Some of you will probably recognize me as Jollie Inch, actor and thespian of stage and screen...
(MUTTERS)
screen and stage. Stage...and screen. Screen...stage...
(SHOUTS)
of *stage* and *screen*!
(Pause)
Prepare yourselves for what may—nay, what will undoubtedly be—a happening. Prepare yourselves now for my latest work, written specifically for you, the audience. I proudly give you my latest creation—
(Pause and then SHOUTS)
Death! of a Quarterback.
(Lays down and covers himself with blankets)

MRS. DANDELION / PEPPY
(From offstage to doctor)

What do we do?

DOCTOR / JUD ROY
(From offstage to Mrs. Dandelion)

Improvise! Improvise! Pretend like Jollie was supposed to announce himself all along. OK—I'm on now.
Doctor enters. A white coat and plastic stethoscope easily identify him. Places stethoscope against Rufus's chest.

RUFUS / JOLLIE
(MOANS)

DOCTOR / JUD ROY
(Leans over and whispers to Rufus)

You're dead, stupid. Don't make any noise until you come back alive and surprise everyone.

MRS. DANDELION / PEPPY
(Enters stage and kneels at the foot of bed. Wrings hands)

DOCTOR / JUD ROY
(Addresses Mrs. Dandelion)

Mrs. Dandelion?

MRS. DANDELION / PEPPY

Yes?

DOCTOR / JUD ROY

Are you Mrs. Dandelion?

MRS. DANDELION / PEPPY
Yes—I am Mrs. Dandelion. I am Mrs. Rufus Dandelion.

DOCTOR / JUD ROY
Have we ever met?

MRS. DANDELION / PEPPY
No—you and I have never met. Never. Not even once.

DOCTOR / JUD ROY
I thought not. Mrs. Dandelion, I am sorry to tell you that, as suspected, your husband lost his mind years ago from repeated head slams. But he is here today because he was grievously injured in the game last week. Our diagnosis is—I, and all of us, are certain, dead certain, that he is certainly dead.

MRS. DANDELION / PEPPY
(Wrings hands)
Oh, Doctor! When I heard he was injured in the game, had there been somebody there to catch me, I would have fainted away. My Rufus—I told him to quit football—how he loved me. And I him!
(Looks out a cardboard frame depicting a window)

DOCTOR / JUD ROY
And how he loved football!
(Long pause)
Funny thing. People dying for the sake of a football game—football, dammit! Greatest game in the world! That's the way I'd want to go!
Bleeding on a muddy field!

MRS. DANDELION / PEPPY
(Steps forward and puts her hand on Doctor's arm)
Thank God his team won.

DOCTOR / JUD ROY
Thank God for that! Rescue Dogs, dammit! Best team in the world!

MRS. DANDELION / PEPPY
(Sobs and wrings hands.)
That morning—it was so scary, but I swear, he knew he was going to die! That it was his last game! As he left, he told me, "I might not be home tonight." It was the first time I ever bet against the Rescue Dogs. Maybe it was bad luck.

DOCTOR / JUD ROY
No—he was meant to go out the way he lived—in a blaze of glory. I didn't want to tell you, but I...I was at the game last week when it happened. All you could hear was the roar of the crowd and the sportscaster's voice screaming, 'Look at that son of a bitch run!' It would have been the last thing he heard. That's the way I'd want to go! Football, dammit! Touchdown! Touchdown! Rufus Dandelion, dammit! Best quarterback in the world!

MRS. DANDELION / PEPPY
He loved crowds. He would have been so bored with just me and you here. You here and I here, I mean.

DOCTOR / JUD ROY
(Puts his hand above his eyes, leans forward, and peeks out an imaginary door)
It's one o'clock—everyone's at lunch.

MRS. DANDELION / PEPPY

In a hospital?

DOCTOR / JUD ROY

The union contract says everyone has to have lunch at one. They had to—the doctors and nurses were so busy with the patients, nobody ever got to eat.

MRS. DANDELION / PEPPY

Understandable. Finally, we can really be alone. Oh, darling! I love you so.

DOCTOR / JUD ROY

Call me "Doctor." His estate? The insurance?

MRS. DANDELION / PEPPY

I have the papers hidden in my underwear drawer, where no one dare look.
(Wrings hands)

DOCTOR / JUD ROY

How much was he worth?

MRS. DANDELION / PEPPY

I'm not sure. A lot. He was worth a lot.

DOCTOR / JUD ROY

How much?

MRS. DANDELION / PEPPY

He was worth a hell of a lot.
(Sees Rufus's girlfriend, played by Leslie, crouched behind a plant)

Who are you? I thought you were an azalea. Why, that orange dress is just the color of a prison jumpsuit. Just who were you looking for, dearie? Perhaps a quarterback?

(Girlfriend tries to speak, but is interrupted by Rufus)

RUFUS / JOLLIE
(Addresses wife)

It is I, your husband, come back from the dead. The woman in the orange dress is my girlfriend. Yes, I was sleeping with other women. You knew. Everybody knew—nobody even tried to keep it a secret.

GIRLFRIEND / LESLIE
(Stands up and addresses Rufus angrily)

You're still supposed to be dead still, remember? So, die, idiot, die!

DOCTOR / JUD ROY
(Leans over Rufus's bed)

Yes. Be dead and end this pain. Such a great, great man. He struggles desperately to return to life, but his brain is so mashed from playing football, he does not know that he is dead. A man of such awesome strength must be bound for his own safety and the safety of others.

Doctor wrestles with and then lays his chest across Rufus, pinning him down. Doctor ties Rufus's wrists with gauze. Mrs. Dandelion and Girlfriend look surprised and then rush forward. Mrs. Dandelion helps the Doctor further bind Rufus's wrists, and Girlfriend ties his ankles. The Grim Reaper hurries in from off stage and assists everyone. Rufus is helplessly tied.

RUFUS / JOLLIE
(Gasps and struggles)

What the hell!

DOCTOR / JUD ROY
(Slams his fist down on Rufus's chest and then tapes
Rufus's mouth with white hospital tape)
His large, dangerous teeth must also be bound!

RUFUS / JOLLIE
(Tires and lays down, but struggles intermittently throughout
the play)

DOCTOR / JUD ROY
Your lines, Leslie! Your lines! Keep going!

GIRLFRIEND / LESLIE
Mrs. Dandelion is right! This dress does looks like a prison
jumpsuit. But what's more important is that I was sleeping with
Rufus Dandelion, but he loved me the best of all his other wom-
en. Rufus, Rufus, my large and feared quarterback, is gone.
Without him by my side, I am lost! Wake up, my dear Rufus!
Wake up!
(She slaps him several times in the face)

RUFUS / JOLLIE
(Sputters and squeaks through the tape)

MRS. DANDELION / PEPPY
Darling, how can I let you go? Speak to me, Rufus—one last time!
(Grasps Rufus's hair with both hands. Roughly lifts and shakes
his head)

RUFUS/JOLLIE
Mmmf...mmmf

DINO / GRIM REAPER

I am your narrator, playing the Grim Reaper. He is almost gone.
Awaken! Awaken, Rufus, so you may die and be reborn!
(She slaps him several times in the face)

A MAN IN THE AUDIENCE

Isn't the Grim Reaper supposed to be skinny?

A WOMAN IN THE AUDIENCE

The Grim Reaper seems to have reaped too much.

MODERATOR and GRIM REAPER / DINO

I alone, will decide whether he lives or dies!
(Skulks around the stage)

RUFUS / JOLLIE

(Makes GROWLING sounds and chews the tape)

GIRLFRIEND / LESLIE

Rufus! Rufus! Come back to me, Rufus!
(Slaps Rufus in the face again)

RUFUS / JOLLIE

(His struggling and growling intensify. He chokes on tape.)

DOCTOR / JUD ROY

(Sees that Rufus is choking and rips tape off.)

RUFUS / JOLLIE
(SCREAMS in pain)
AHHHHHHH!

DOCTOR / JUD ROY
Jollie! Jollie! Can you breathe? Are you all right, Jollie?

RUFUS / JOLLIE
(Angrily to doctor)
You son of a bitch!

DOCTOR / JUD ROY
Lines, Jollie! Lines!

MRS. DANDELION / PEPPY
(Wrings hands)
He lives! He lives!

GIRLFRIEND / LESLIE
Thanks be to God! He is strong and mighty still!

RUFUS / JOLLIE
(Remembers audience, lies down, and calms himself.
To Mrs. Dandelion)
Bury me with my helmet on.

MRS. DANDELION / PEPPY
Suit or uniform?

RUFUS / JOLLIE
(In a weak voice)
The Armani Suit—with my Hermes tie. One thing more before I
die. The ugly lady in the prison jumpsuit is my one great love, and
I, hers. I am leaving all my money and signed football memorabilia
to her. Contact my attorney, Sam Smolinski-Pekorskivich, and he
will present my true will.

(He gives a ghostly MOAN and closes his eyes.)
UHHHHHH. Jud Roy, I die happy knowing that I will haunt
you forever.

MRS. DANDELION / PEPPY
(Wrings hands)
He dies! He dies! He's dead now, right?

(Looks at DOCTOR / JUD ROY)
DOCTOR / JUD ROY
Yes, he is dead—he is dead at last. Thanks be to God!

MODERATOR and GRIM REAPER / DINO
Now, we can pray.
(She embraces Peppy, who pulls away.)

GIRLFRIEND / LESLIE
(Desperately)
Rufus. Rufus, come back to me! How do you spell "Smolinski-
Pekorskivich?" And is it "Sam" or "Samuel?"

DOCTOR / JUD ROY
(Puts his arm around Leslie/Rufus's girlfriend)
My dear, how pretty you are when you cry.

PERSON IN AUDIENCE
When did she start crying?

DOCTOR / JUD ROY
Rufus must have loved you very much to leave you all that money. You
may be assured, lovely lady, that I will stay by your side and protect
you from any evil people who would dare try and steal it from you.

GIRLFRIEND / LESLIE
I believe you! Love comes to all, even someone like me!

DOCTOR / JUD ROY
Yes, I could even love someone like you.

MRS. DANDELION / PEPPY
Ah, love. It is a many splendored thing. But he's my husband, so the money's still mine.

DOCTOR / JUD ROY
That's not in the play. Stop trying to show off, Peppy.

RUFUS / JOLLIE
(Shouting)
You're going to jail for assault, Jud Roy!

DOCTOR / JUD ROY
(Shouting back)
The ghost of Rufus Dandelion threatens! But I care nothing about going to jail. I will kill your wife, marry your girlfriend, and take all of your money! Ah-ha!
>(Doctor grabs Mrs. Dandelion and shakes her. Gracefully, she lies on the floor, sighing and wringing her hands.)

I die, I die!

MODERATOR and GRIM REAPER / DINO
(Points at Mrs. Dandelion.)
And now, cheating wife, you may join your cheating husband!

MRS. DANDELION / PEPPY
(SCREAMS)
EEEEEK!

Why, it's the Grim Reaper, again! No, no death, be gone! (Grim Reaper / Moderator takes Mrs. Dandelion's hand. Gracefully, Mrs. Dandelion stands. She adjusts her underwear.)

GRIM REAPER / DINO
(Walks off stage, leading Mrs. Dandelion by the hand.)

MRS. DANDELION / PEPPY
It's not fair! I'm the wife, so that money's mine! And Rufus cheated on me, too!

GIRLFRIEND / LESLIE
She is gone. And what she said wasn't in the play either.

DOCTOR / JUD ROY
Just stick to the lines, Leslie. You're really doing very well. Yes, my dear. Her soul is gone.

RUFUS / JOLLIE
Her body was so beautiful that they took it too.

DOCTOR / JUD ROY
But a black heart. Jollie, you died again, so shut up.

RUFUS / JOLLIE
She was an unfaithful trollop, but I loved her, and I feel bad she is dead! Jud Roy, if you don't untie me, you'll be dead too.

DOCTOR / JUD ROY
Everyone! Listen to me! There is no dead quarterback here—because a quarterback like Rufus Dandelion will live forever! I can almost hear his voice.

GIRLFRIEND / LESLIE

So can I. He would have wanted it that way.

The doctor and Rufus's girlfriend gaze at one another. Crash of cymbals. The stage lights turn from white to red to blue and then to white again. Rufus still struggles to free himself. The rest of the Three Musketeers walk backstage.

MODERATOR / DINO

(Returns and takes center stage)

And so ends the sad saga of Rufus, who died at the height of his career. Also, Mrs. Dandelion died too, but Rufus was the important one. Um, I am Dino Quiet Room, your moderator—

RUFUS / JOLLIE

(Finally frees himself and sits up)

DINO

(Frightened, runs backstage.)

The End!

Jollie climbed down off the bed. Anyone could see that he was hugely pissed off. The play sucked, and Jud Roy had made a fool of him. He stood on the stage, glaring, not knowing quite what to do. The others walked out from backstage, formed a line, and prepared to bow. Instead of joining them, Jollie stepped directly in front. Jud Roy, Dino, Peppy, and Leslie froze. Jollie's hospital gown was open in the back, and he was not wearing underwear. His naked posterior twinkled in the stage lights. Jollie made four bows to the audience and then turned around and made a low bow to Jud Roy, Dino, Peppy, and Leslie. The audience gasped.

Finally, he turned toward the audience again and waved, shouting, "Thank you—thank you all. My name is Jollie Inch—remember—Jollie

Inch is my name. It should be Jollie Inch*es*, but heh, heh, heh—take warning, ladies! God bless—and good night!"

A loud noise in the back! The double doors of the auditorium slammed open. Two big-shouldered police officers entered, and everyone stopped what they were doing to watch.

"No one leave!" ordered the officer with the blond hair.

"Stay right where you are!" yelled the officer with the black hair.

"Is there a Leslie Tomatiny here?" the blond officer shouted.

"Come out with your hands up!" boomed the dark-haired officer.

The two police officers rushed onto the stage. The blond officer shoved the Three Musketeers aside and made an announcement.

"We have a report from Allmart Supervisor Gene Pimpernel that a Leslie Tomatiny, escaped criminal at large, stole several valuable items from Allmart. She admitted her guilt in front of several witnesses and two security officers. We are here to arrest her for theft, fleeing justice, and other violations to be announced."

"But she didn't do it!" yelled a deep voice from the back.

The dark-haired officer stood tall. "Shut up, deep voice from the back. This is a police matter. Interfere again, and I will throw you in jail, henceforth!"

"There's no need to throw anyone in jail but me. I am Leslie Tomatiny," Leslie announced. She held her out her hands to be cuffed. The blond officer moved toward her.

"Wait!" the same deep voice from the back bellowed.

It was Larger Billie. He had snuck in while Jollie was taking his bows. The fat man ran panting toward the stage. The blond officer let go of Leslie and backed away. He shouted at Larger Billie.

"Stop! Stop! Stop, or I'll shoot—Really, I will, I really will, you'd better stop, I mean it, now, stop, or I swear to God, I'll shoot you, OK?"

Larger Billie was almost to the stage.

Now, the dark-haired officer gave the orders.

"OK, he really means it this time. I've known this guy a long time, and you'd better stop. He's an animal, I tell you—he's crazy! Don't be stupid. It's not worth it."

Larger Billie began climbing the stairs up to the stage.

The blond-haired officer wanted to negotiate.

"Hold on now, just hold on there. Let's talk about it. You and me. Tell me all about yourself. I'm a good listener. Just settle down, relax, and we'll talk. You don't want to die. Think of your mother."

Larger Billie was on the stage.

The dark-haired officer jumped back, lost his balance, and skittered sideways, crashing into Leslie. Leslie stumbled and would have landed flat on her butt had Larger Billie not grabbed her. He held her up and gazed into her eyes.

"Leslie—Leslie, are you all right?"

"Yes, Larger. I'm all right, but this may be the last time we ever see one another. I never stole from Allmart, but nobody will believe me. None of this is your fault, Billie. It's just my life. It's just me. And it always will be. The best thing is for me to go to jail and hope you'll wait for me."

Larger shook her. "Leslie! Listen to me! It's all right! I have proof—this photo's from the surveillance tape at Allmart. See, that bushy-haired guy with tattoos is putting stuff in your purse—"

"I know that man! That's the guy who sleeps with my mother!" Leslie shrieked.

"Yes! It's your mother's roommate. Or was. By the way, your mother died and left you her house."

"But, why?" asked Leslie. "Tell me why."

"Because you were her daughter and she died before marrying anyone she really liked, thank God," said Larger Billy.

"I mean, why would her roommate do such a thing?"

"He hated you, Leslie. When you moved, your mother refused to let him have your room. He slept on the couch until the day she died... also, he knew that you would throw him out of the house after your mother died."

"He slept on the couch until the day she died? That's a lot of sleeping. I moved out almost a year ago," said Leslie thoughtfully.

"Yes, I wondered about that too. Anyways, when he saw you at Allmart, he slipped the stuff in your purse, hoping you would go to jail and he could stay," said Billie. "He told me everything after I threatened to break his legs."

"A likely story!" sneered the blond police officer. Both officers stood awkwardly next to Leslie and Larger Billie.

Larger Billie shoved the photo into his face. "Here's the evidence, jerk! The picture's right there—that's the guy putting stuff in Leslie's purse. Why don't you go and arrest him? He's here in Oakland, at the Hot Hog Hotel on 3456 Asphalt Road, living in a coffee shop stoop he has no intention of paying for."

The dark-haired officer examined the photo. "Perhaps we'd better investigate this further," he said.

"We'll have to get the forensic lab to examine this photograph carefully," said the blond-haired officer. He nodded to Leslie. "We may have to speak with you further, ma'am."

The two men shuffled out. Leslie never heard from them again.

Leslie stared up at Larger Billie. Her eyes glazed over and a tear rolled down her cheek and off her chin.

"Larger!" Leslie cried and flung her arms open wide.

Larger Billie threw one arm around her back, the other arm under her legs, and lifted her up. Leslie put her arms around his neck and rested her head on his chest. They stayed that way, their hearts beating furiously.

Everyone loved the surprise ending. Overwhelmed by the appearance of the police, the horror of the crime, and the lover's display of emotion, the audience stood as one and gave the players a standing ovation. One man even yelled, "Bravo!" which made him look like a fool.

Dino turned toward the audience. "Thank you again for joining us for *Death of a Quarterback*, starring Jollie Inch as Rufus Dandelion, Jud Roy Lebowitz as the doctor, Peppy Zipline as Rufus's wife, Leslie, who was first Rufus's girlfriend and then the doctor's and then the fat man's. Oh—and I am Dino Quiet Room, your moderator and death."

Larger Billie and the Three Musketeers threw kisses and walked backstage. The smiling audience left the auditorium, and the Three Musketeers joined Mr. Bottomly in front of the stage.

CHAPTER 29

Fame and True Love

● ● ●

MR. BOTTOMLY SAT SPRAWLED IN a chair, his head in his hands. *He showed his bare bottom—to the PTA, no less! It was Jud Roy's fault. Jud Roy was in charge of the entire damn thing.* Behind the patch, his wandering eye leapt back and forth like a caged animal.

"Well, Superintendent—how did you like it?" asked Jud Roy.

Mr. Bottomly turned his red face to the professor. "What the hell was that? Something highbrow! Classy! 'Adult entertainment' does not mean a horse's ass!" He was weeping sweat.

Jud Roy threw up his hands in disbelief. "What is this I'm hearing? Are you kidding? That was a standing ovation!"

Jollie looked at them all calmly. "Although I still intend to pursue a civil suit against him, for once Jud Roy and I agree. The audience was very impressed. They gave the very reaction I expected and deserved. You may not be aware of this Mr. Bottomly, but adult entertainment can be many things. I thought it a masterpiece. Highbrow? There is nothing more highbrow than the combination of art and nudity. Think of Pablo Picasso's deformed naked ladies. Think of Paul Ruben's fat naked ladies. Think of all the naked ladies in movies."

"Fat ladies in a movie naked?" Peppy asked incredulously.

Mr. Bottomly wasn't thinking about fat ladies in a movie naked. He pointed a shaking finger at Jud Roy.

"Jud Roy, this is your fault! Talented students, my ass—excuse my language. I was a sailor not so long ago. Jud Roy, if this is going to result in my unemployment, if this is going to cost me my job, it's going to cost you yours even more! I shall begin the complicated process of firing you the first thing tomorrow—no matter how long, no matter how many forms or meetings it takes, you will be ousted! Let go! You will be absolutely discharged with no uncertain haste! I remind you that, except for during the Bay to Breakers race, the Gay Pride Parade, The Mardi Gras, and the Folsom Street Fair, public nudity is illegal in this state!"

Mr. Bottomly glanced at Larger Billie and Leslie, who were smiling and holding hands. "However, the romance was a nice touch," he admitted.

Jud Roy looked sick. "Superintendent Bottomly, I have already met with several students who are very interested in taking my next class. Six of them have submitted samples of their work and, I assure you, their talent is irrefutable—most remarkable, in fact. As to this evening's performance, I believe the nudity may have been too advanced for a collection of ordinary, middle-class parents whose idea of entertainment is to sleep in a tent in the backyard."

"Right!" Jollie agreed.

A woman who had snuck in quietly approached the group.

"Ms. Fineworth!" Larger Billie greeted her. "Everyone, this is Ms. Fineworth, curator of LMNO, the Livermore Museum Now Open. We met at Secureway. She came into the store looking for Leslie." Larger Billie seemed excited about seeing Ms. Fineworth.

"I couldn't find her anywhere. There are a surprising number of grocery stores in Livermore. Nice to see you again, my dear." Carlotta fluttered her hands.

"Uh—it's been quite a while, Ms. Fineworth," said Leslie awkwardly.

Ms. Fineworth sighed into her age. Her eyes softened as she looked at Leslie. Once in a while, she met someone like this young woman who reminded her that she had never had children. The curator reached out and grasped Leslie's hand.

"Ms. Tomatiny, is has been a while—it was rude of me not to call you about exhibiting your work. The fact is that, at first Livermore Museum

Now Open was struggling so for money, we could barely pay for heat! We couldn't have even paid for the fruit for one of your marvelous displays. But as it turned out, that stupid LMNO nickname drew so many children to the museum, we've actually begun to turn a healthy profit. Field trips, tourists, holiday outings—families and schools from all over the bay area come to LMNO. Livermore has changed so much. We have a theater there, now...not a movie house, but a theater with live people from all over the world—and restaurants that are so busy, you have to make reservations! There are fountains, art galleries and wineries, really pretty ones that give away free wine. Ms. Tomatiny, please consider doing an exhibit for LMNO—I know the children would just love your fruit displays—of course, they must be appropriate. You would have to use a more suitable vegetable than zucchini. We can negotiate the details and your fees—perhaps next week?"

"Leslie!" cried Larger Billie. "You're going to be a real artist! With pay!"

"Oh, Larger!" She snuggled her face against Larger Billie's shoulder. "I've so missed you. Now that my mother is dead and I have a house, I can move back to Livermore and make fruit displays."

"Ms. Tomatiny, I truly hope you will move back to Livermore. I think I misjudged you," smiled Carlotta.

"Thank you, Ms. Fineworth. I've got lots of ideas for new displays—"

Jud Roy interrupted. "Shut up, Leslie!" He didn't want to hear any good news. What he needed to feel better was someone worse off than he was.

Larger Billie shook a fist at the professor. "You speak like that to my lady again, I'll squash you like the cockroach you are," he threatened.

Jud Roy didn't even hear him. "Mr. Bottomly! I mean, Superintendent Bottomly! Listen, Jollie sprung his butt on us without any warning at all. Superintendent, if you're going to have someone arrested, arrest him! I didn't have anything to do with it."

Jollie smoothed his Hermes tie against the hospital gown. "Nudity, indeed. One day, my work will be recognized. Perhaps this very school will be named after me, instead of that Fillmore nobody. People will be standing in line to see me naked."

"You nincompoop! Millard Fillmore was not a nobody! He was president of the United States!" yelled Mr. Bottomly.

Leslie knew some interesting facts about President Fillmore. "As a young man, Millard Fillmore bred horses. He led a mob that captured and hung the notorious horse thief, Justin Le Barge. A book, 'True Grits of the West' describes the incident in graphic detail."

Jud Roy didn't care about cowboy justice. "Shut up, Leslie! What would a California girl know about grits? You don't even know where Scandinavia is!"

This time, Larger Billie grabbed Jud Roy by the collar and threw him against the wall. The professor bounced back and barely managed to stay on his feet.

"It is indeed high time someone gave that blackguard what he deserves. Good work, sir! Capital work!" said Mr. Bottomly to Larger Billie.

"Nice going, Leslie—you got yourself a real man, there." Peppy said. She rested her hand on Larger Billie's arm. He jerked it away and kissed Leslie gently on the head.

"Sir, what was your name again?" asked Mr. Bottomly.

"William—Larger William," said Larger Billie proudly.

"I sure do love that tie, Jollie," said Peppy, smiling.

Jollie did not answer. He was getting sick of chasing after someone who was vainer than he was. Besides, Peppy wasn't going to come around. Seeing Leslie and Larger Billie together made him realize that.

Peppy turned away from Jollie and smiled into Mr. Bottomly's eyes. The supervisor felt lost and found at the same time, and he lowered his voice to a manly rumble.

"Excuse me, Peppy, for your having to witness my earlier rough behavior. It was beastly, so caveman-like, well, brutish, really."

"I rather enjoyed it," said Peppy brightly.

He went on. "Of course you did, my dear. A beautiful woman often enjoys men vying for her attention, for it is nature's way of selecting which man will win her charms—but fisticuffs? It's upset you, gentle flower. And what woman wouldn't be upset having to deal with these false fools?"

"Will I see you later?" Peppy asked Mr. Bottomly. At the same time, she glanced toward Jud Roy, who glared back. She turned and stared up at Mr. Bottomly.

"How I wish I could, but—I have laundry to do tonight." He lowered his voice to barely a whisper.

"Perhaps I could help?" suggested Peppy.

"Why, yes. Yes indeed! We could dine out first—somewhere new. There's a new French restaurant in the city—Bistro Da Day. It's supposed to be excellent."

"Oh yes, Superintendent Bottomly. That would be lovely," said Peppy.

Mr. Bottomly and Peppy walked out together, followed by Dino, Leslie, and Larger Billie. Once outside, Peppy tried to take his arm, but Mr. Bottomly thought that such public displays of affection were improper for a superintendent.

Jollie hung back. He hated seeing Larger and Leslie, and Bottomly and Peppy together. Jud Roy had hidden his clothes, so Jollie threw a coat on over the hospital gown and stomped passed them to his car. His tires screeched as he roared away.

Jollie leaned as far out as he could from the cloud. This was the best part. Snuggling into the white fluff, he waited for the shock of the explosion, the blinding light, and the excitement of the fire. Ah! There it was. The heat! The french-fry smell! And how the explosion made the buildings rattle!

Mr. Bottomly, Peppy, Dino, and what was left of the audience stared from the parking lot, mesmerized by the fiery display.

"Jollie prophesized he would die, and so he has," said Dino knowingly.

"Kind of hot out here," commented Mr. Bottomly.

Jollie sighed from the cloud. "I can almost feel the flames—and there's that fool, Jud Roy, being chased by Larger Billie. Incredible finish!"

It was one hell of a show.

CHAPTER 30

Unexpected Guests

● ● ●

JOLLIE STARTLED AND NEARLY FELL out of his cloud. There was something there—soft, piddy paws were reaching out of the cloud floor. A tiny kitten struggled out of a hole in the cloud. When it finally escaped, it patted boldly over to Jollie and curled up in his lap. Its body was warm and alive. It had a heartbeat and the soft sound of breath in its nose. It had been a long time since Jollie had touched a living thing. Tentatively, he patted the kitten. It purred, gave a barely audible mew, and went to sleep.

Jollie sensed something larger behind him. He whirled his head around and jumped up. The kitten fell unharmed into the cloud.

What the hell is Jud Roy doing here!

Jud Roy stood calmly, looking very old and very tired. Like Jollie, he wore a standard hospital gown.

"Excuse me. Is this Cloud I? I gotta message for I."

"Jud Roy—are you...dead?"

"Jollie! You're still here? Yeah, I've been dead almost ten years. Heart attack—I went fast."

"Boring way to go, but effective enough, I suppose," said Jollie.

"Let's try this again," said Jud Roy, "I was sent here. With a message for I."

"You were sent with a message for yourself?" asked Jollie.

"A message for you, fool. The message is, 'Get rid of the cat.'"

"What cat?" Jollie asked innocently. He picked up the kitten and tried to hide it in his hospital gown.

Before Jollie could stop him, Jud Roy grabbed the kitten and threw it out the arched opening. The two watched the outspread silhouette of a cat scream toward the earth. The kitten sprawled out on top of a zucchini plant in a communal garden in Berkeley, where it died and was reincarnated into a potato bug. It bumbled away, seemingly content.

"You bastard!" Jollie screamed. "I just got that cat!"

"I'd have recognized her anywhere," Jud Roy commented.

"Recognized who?"

"Dino, you fool. She died a minute ago and turned into a cat," Jud Roy said. "And you let her sit in your lap!"

Jollie had never felt so sad. "Why can't I have a cat? I love cats. Even if it is Dino, why shouldn't she stay?"

Jud Roy gave Jollie a tired look. "Dino doesn't belong here. We don't discriminate based on religion, but species is another thing entirely. I gotta go. Just stopped by to deliver a message from the 'thing' upstairs." Jud Roy shivered. "I gotta go."

"Go where? Where you going, Jud Roy? Wait a minute! What happened to Leslie and Larger Billie? What happened to Peppy? And Mr. Bottomly?"

"Bottomly and Peppy? I never knew. Leslie and Larger Billie moved to Livermore, and Leslie got a write-up in *Persons Magazine* about those fruit things she does. So far as I know, they're both still there." He looked thoughtful. "You know what? Sometime before you died, I looked up Scandinavia. Leslie was right. It isn't a country. I never told her I knew. I never told anyone, but she was right."

"I feel bad about that," Jollie said thoughtfully.

"Yeah, me too," said Jud Roy. He jumped and then leaned back and called up to the sky. "I'll be right up, just finishing here, found an old friend. Heh, heh—well, you know how these things can be, you just get to talking—"

He was gone.

Jollie sighed, sat down, and stared at the cupcake button. He felt something under his hand. A plump, wiggly little creature with a hideous face was struggling out of a tangled tunnel in the cloud. Jollie looked down at the potato bug. He patted his knee, and the potato bug climbed up and settle in. "It's you and me, Dino," he said, gently stroking the insect's hideous head.

Jollie hesitated a moment to let his hand float above the cupcake button before pressing it. He felt the cloud jerk forward, and his heart vaulted into his throat. Dino held on tight, riding his knee. Fast as they traveled, the world was a long, long way off.

End

Made in the
USA
Middletown, DE